The Handy Helpers

I like Spike
You will too.

Rosemary
Heddens

The Handy Helpers

Book Three

Red, White, and . . . Bloopers!

Rosemary Morgan Heddens

Rev. date: 11/06/2014

Xlibris
1-888-795-4274
www.Xlibris.com
540411

To the original Spike,
my son, Michael

CHAPTER ONE

Jennifer stared in shock at the contents of her cereal bowl. "Mom!" she yelled. "Mom, come here!"

"What . . . What . . . What is it?" Carolyn Smith tried to catch her breath after running down the stairs. "What's wrong?"

"There's a dead mouse in my cereal!" Jennifer screamed. "Just look!"

Michael, Jennifer's younger brother, had come running into the kitchen behind their mother. "That's a rat, not a mouse," Michael informed her matter-of-factly. "And it's not real."

"It has hair on it!" Jennifer insisted, still upset. "It looks real to me!"

Michael lifted the rubber rat out of the bowl by its tail and brushed away crumbs of cereal. "Name's Chuck. Chuck's a high-quality fake rat. He cost me five dollars."

"What's he doing in the cereal box?" his mother demanded to know.

"Dad only lets us have one box of cereal a week. Jennifer and Monica eat a big bowl every day until it's gone. I hardly get any. I thought when they saw Chuck, they wouldn't want the cereal."

"I realize having a dentist for a dad isn't the easiest thing in the world, but terrifying your family with fake rodents isn't the answer!"

"I won't do it again. I promise." Michael tucked Chuck into the pocket of his shorts—beady eyes peeking out.

"I'm afraid that's not good enough this time," his mother said. "I warned you what would happen if you didn't stop with these practical jokes. We're all tired of them!"

"I said I won't do it again," Michael repeated. "I'm s'posed to meet Chris and Logan. We're going fishing."

"Not today you're not!" Carolyn stepped between him and the back door. "Today you're going to pay your dues for your don'ts!"

"Now you sound like Amber's mom," Michael groaned loudly.

"Yeah, well, she has the right idea," Carolyn said, seriously. "You have to be held accountable for the choices you make."

"So am I grounded?" Michael asked.

"In a way, yes," Carolyn continued. "Instead of going fishing today, you're going to wash all the windows on the outside of the house."

That'll take hours," Michael whined.

"And that will give you plenty of time to consider what you've done!" Carolyn said as the final word on the subject.

Michael had barely gotten the cleaning supplies set out in front of the first window when his mother came out the door with her purse slung over her shoulder.

"I'm volunteering at the church office today," she told Michael. "I expect to see sparkling windows when I return."

"Don't worry, Mom. I've got this under control. You'll be happy when you get home." He watched as his mother got into her Escalade and backed out of the driveway.

Just as Michael was getting ready to spray window cleaner on the first window, his friends Chris and Logan came riding up on their bikes. There was fishing gear sticking out of their bike bags. The two boys were about the same height, a head taller than Spike, but Logan appeared to be slimmer. This could have been due to the fact that he always wore his shirt tucked in and Chris, as usual, was dressed in oversize shirt and shorts. Logan wore his light-brown hair in a crew cut, which gave him a tidy appearance. Chris liked his brown hair longer and combed down over his forehead. His casual look made him seem more easygoing than his sometimes-uptight friend.

"Hey, Spike, aren't you going fishing?" Logan shouted as he parked his bike in the driveway. (Even though his name was Michael, his friends all called him Spike because he spiked his hair and held it in place with lots of gel. Sometimes he even sprayed the spiked hair with red or purple hairspray.)

"I have to wash all the windows first," Spike told his friends. "Maybe you'd like to give me a hand."

"Is washing the windows a chore or a punishment?" Chris asked.

"It was just a little practical joke," Spike said. "I don't know why my mom went all ballistic like that!"

"You're on your own." Logan laughed. "We're going fishing."

"Yeah," Chris added. "Your mom's no one to mess with!"

Chris and Logan got back on their bikes and rode away toward Fox Creek, where they hoped the fish would be biting. Spike returned to cleaning the windows. "Maybe I can join you later!" He called after his friends, who were now almost out of sight.

Spike let out a long sigh and surveyed what seemed like an endless row of windows. This job was going to take all morning. Two seven-year-olds, Connor and his friend, Blake, walked across the lawn to the front porch where Spike was wiping the window. Just like Spike, Connor had his hair spiked. And just like Spike, Connor liked to wear shirts with sayings on them. Today he was wearing a T-shirt that said "Being Cool is my Job."

"Whatcha doin'?" Connor asked. "Did your mom make you wash windows?"

"My mom *make* me?" Spike gave Connor a shocked look. "My mom didn't make me. My mom *let* me wash the windows. I asked her—in fact, I practically begged her to let me wash windows."

"Why'd you do that?" Connor asked.

"'Cause washing windows is about the most fun thing you can do on a summer morning. You get to spray water, and no one will yell at you. Then you get to use these cool window-cleaner bottles, see?

"Can we help you?" Blake asked. "We're looking for something fun to do."

"I don't know," Spike said thoughtfully. "I was thinking about keeping all this fun for myself."

"Please," Connor begged. "Let us help. I'll give you half my candy bar."

"Well . . . maybe," Spike said casually. "I guess it might be worth half a candy bar. But just you, okay?"

"What about me?" Blake asked. His dark eyes flashed under his baseball cap. "Can I help too?"

"Well . . . What've you got?" Spike questioned.

"I have almost a whole pack of gum," Blake offered, taking the gum from the pocket of his tan shorts.

"Okay," Spike said, snatching up the gum, "you can both help."

Connor and Blake grabbed the cleaning supplies and started on the next window. Spike took out a piece of gum and popped it in his mouth. Then he stood back, chewing the gum and watching the other two. "There's a streak right there," he pointed out to Blake.

Just as the pair finished wiping the window, a girl named Madison came by to see what was going on. After paying Spike a quarter, she joined the other two at the next window. Before long, there were five little kids washing the windows. Spike was feeling pretty pleased with himself. This was the best plan he'd ever devised. The windows were being cleaned by little gnomes, and he was free to do whatever he wanted. Maybe he would take a nap or watch TV.

"Michael David Smith!" His mother's voice made him jump.

"What's going on here?"

"I . . . I . . . I thought you were working in the church office?" Michael stammered.

"I just came back to get something. I was expecting to see *you* washing the windows!"

"They begged me to let them help," Spike tried to explain. "I didn't have the heart to tell them no."

"Washing windows is fun," Connor defended Spike. "That's why Spike let us do it. He's a nice guy."

"I wouldn't exactly say that," Spike said to his mom.

"Neither would I!" Carolyn stormed. "You kids put down the cleaning supplies and go home. Washing the windows is Michael's job!"

"But I paid him a quarter," Madison whined.

"You took money from these kids?" Carolyn glared at her son. "You give it all back right now!"

Spike was just finishing the last window when Chris and Logan returned from their fishing trip. "Catch anything?" Spike asked, hoping they would say no.

"We caught a couple of small ones," Chris opened the ice chest to show him two trout. "Logan's going to take them home. He said his mom will fix them for dinner. It's not enough for my big family."

"It looks like you finished your window washing," Logan said. "Too bad you missed the fishing though."

"That's okay," Spike tried to sound unconcerned. "I've got the whole summer to go fishing."

"But not tomorrow," Logan reminded him. "Tomorrow we're helping Beth Anne's family move into their new house."

"I'll be there," Spike promised. "What time are we supposed to show up?"

"The moving van is getting there at eight," Logan said. "We should probably be there about that time too."

Spike was gathering up the cleaning supplies when his sister Jennifer rode up in Todd Jensen's old brown Ford Bronco. She was already sporting a great summer tan, set off by her white shorts and red strappy sandals. Her dark-brown hair was pulled up off her neck and tied into a knot in the back. A few loose strands streamed down both sides of her face. Todd, whose blond hair was usually longer, had gotten a buzz cut for the summer. He was dressed in cutoff jeans and a light-blue T-shirt. Todd walked around to the passenger side and opened the door for Jennifer. Then the two came up the walk hand in hand.

Spike said "Yuck" under his breath when he saw Todd. Jennifer had been dating Todd for two months. Three months was her usual time limit with a boyfriend, so Spike figured she would be dumping Todd soon. At least, he was hoping she would.

Jennifer and Todd had just finished their junior year at Bluesky High School. In the fall, they would be seniors. Then she would be off to college. Todd would be out of the picture by then for sure.

Jennifer headed into the house, but Todd remained on the porch with Spike. "Whatcha doin', shrimp?" Todd asked, flicking Spike's ear with his finger.

"Ouch!" Spike yelped. "That hurt."

"That didn't hurt." Todd flicked his ear again even harder. "Now that hurt!"

"Leave me alone," Spike groaned, "or I'll tell Jennifer."

"Go ahead," Todd said, tauntingly. "Go crying to your sister, you whiny baby!"

Jennifer came out the door with some CDs in her hands. "Tell Mom I'm over at Margo's listening to music, okay?"

"Tell her yourself!" Spike shot back. Then he got up and ran in the house.

"Your brother's got a smart mouth," Todd said as Spike was leaving.

"Yeah," Jennifer agreed. "He can be a real pain!"

"Don't make any plans for Saturday," Carolyn told her son at dinner that night.

"Why?" Spike let out a big sigh. "Am I still in trouble?"

"I want you to mow the lawn, front and back. The Thomases are coming over for a barbecue on Sunday. I want the yard to look nice."

"I heard you pulled a Tom Sawyer today," Spike's dad, David Smith, said with a grin.

"Who's Tom Sawyer?" Spike asked. "I don't know any kid named Tom Sawyer."

"He's a character in a Mark Twain novel," Monica, Spike's other sister, explained. "Haven't you ever read *The Adventures of Tom Sawyer*?"

"I just finished the fourth grade," Spike reminded her. "We didn't read that book in the fourth grade."

"Well, you should read it," his mother encouraged. "It has a boy in it who's a lot like you. His Aunt Polly told him to whitewash the fence, but he got a bunch of little kids to pay him to let them do it, just like you did with the window washing."

"Yeah," Monica added, "but Tom Sawyer got away with it."

"I don't think he should read that book," David said, trying to sound serious.

"Why not?" Carolyn asked.

"It might give him ideas." David laughed. "He comes up with enough pranks on his own. He doesn't really need any help."

"Good point!" Monica gave her dad a high five.

Lisa Riley pulled out the sofa bed for her daughter Beth Anne. Together, they put on the sheets. "This is the last night you'll be sleeping on the sofa bed," she said. "Tomorrow night you'll be sleeping in your own room in our new home."

"I know," Beth Anne groaned.

"Why the long face?" her mother asked. "I thought you'd be happy about having your own room."

"I am," Beth Anne said, still groaning. "It's just my leg itches in this cast. I wish it was off."

"You only have a week to go, and then the doctor will be taking it off."

"I wish it was today. Having a cast is no fun. I can't ride my bike or go places with my friends."

"I bet you won't go climbing any more hills by yourself or chasing after lost dogs."

"I won't," Beth Anne promised. "I learned my lesson. I won't go any place without telling you first."

"That was a painful lesson to learn, wasn't it?" Lisa tapped her daughter's cast.

"Yes, I made a mistake. But God made it okay. That's what it says on this card Grandma gave me."

Beth Anne handed the card to her mother, who read it out loud. "'We know that all things work for good for those who love God, who are called according to his purpose. Romans eight twenty-eight.'"

"Grandma told me what it means," Beth Anne continued. "It means that even if we do something wrong, God will make it right."

"Yes, he will." Her mother smiled. "According to his purpose."

"What is his purpose?" Beth Anne asked.

"He has a different purpose for each of his children," Lisa explained. "When we live according to God's purpose, things will always turn out right, even if it seems like things are going wrong. Do you understand?"

"Maybe," Beth Anne said. "But I'm not sure. I don't know what my purpose is."

"Just do your best every day, and God will show you his plan for you when he's ready."

Beth Anne lay down on the sofa bed, and her mother brought the covers up to her chin.

"What's the matter now?" Lisa questioned her daughter, who was fidgeting under the covers.

"My leg itches again," Beth Anne moaned. "I wish I could scratch it."

"Soon," her mother reminded her.

"Then I can go swimming," Beth Anne smiled.

"Go swimming? Is there a pool in Bluesky?"

"There has to be a pool so I can practice for Special Olympics."

"I'm not sure they have Special Olympics here," Lisa said thoughtfully.

"There has to be Special Olympics!" Beth Anne insisted. "There just has to be!"

"I'll check into it next week and see what I can find out." Lisa kissed her daughter good night.

CHAPTER TWO

"Where are you going so early in the morning?" Cody Peterson questioned his daughter, who was on her way out the door.

"We're helping Beth Anne move into her new house today. Mom knows all about it," Melissa called out over her shoulder.

"Are you going dressed like that?" Cody pointed to Melissa's jeans that had large holes from midthigh to her knees.

"What's wrong with these jeans?"

"The poor kids in Afghanistan dress better than that. Those pants are full of holes. They look awful!"

"These are expensive jeans. It costs extra for the holes."

"You've got to be kidding!"

"No, I'm not. Everybody wears jeans like these."

"I doubt that. Anyway, go change, or you're not leaving the house!"

"Ugh," Melissa groaned, almost running into her friend Laura, who was about to knock on Melissa's door.

"What's wrong?" Laura asked.

"Nothing," Melissa sighed loudly. "I just wish my dad would hurry up and get a job. Then he won't be around so much."

"I thought you were hoping you would be able to spend more time with him now that he's back from serving in the army in Afghanistan," Laura said.

"Yeah, I did say that, but that was before I knew he was going to try to control my whole life!"

"He's just being a dad," Laura pointed out. "He hasn't done it for quite a while, so he's out of practice."

"Well, he's not out of practice when it comes to bossing me around. In fact, he's an expert!"

Laura and Melissa rode their bikes to Amber's house. Amber was just finishing her breakfast when her friends arrived. Like her friends, she was wearing shorts, a T-shirt, and sneakers.

"We're going to be late," Laura pointed out.

"Sorry," Amber said. "My alarm didn't go off."

"You probably forgot to set it," Laura scolded.

"So what if I did? I don't have your perfect memory. I have attention deficit disorder, you know!"

"This is going to be a fun day," Laura stated sarcastically.

"Why do you say that?" Melissa asked.

"Because both of you obviously got up on the wrong side of the bed," Laura groaned as they walked out the door and to their bikes.

As with Logan, Chris, and Spike, the three girls had just finished the fourth grade. Even so, Melissa was half a foot taller than her two friends. As usual, her blond hair was pulled back and held in place by a flower. Her summer tan set off her azure eyes. Laura kept her brown hair short because it was easier when she did gymnastics. Today, her baseball cap was replaced by a simple visor to keep the sun off her face. Amber's shoulder-length, thick, bronze-colored hair provided the perfect frame for her peaches-and-cream skin and big round brown eyes.

The moving van was just pulling up in front of the Rileys' new home when the girls came riding up on their bikes. "Glad you could make it," Spike said, looking at his watch.

"It doesn't look like we've missed anything," Melissa pointed out.

"No," Logan said, "we're just waiting for instructions from the Rileys. They're inside taking some measurements."

Just then, Beth Anne came out the front door. The cast on her left leg kept her from running to her friends. "I haven't seen you for so long!" she exclaimed.

"It's just been a few days," Melissa pointed out, "since our Handy Helper meeting last Monday."

Two big, burly men dressed in blue pants and gray shirts stepped out of the moving van. The names on their shirts announced to everyone that they were Jack and Alan. Jack rolled up the back of the moving van and pulled out a ramp. Alan lifted out a hand truck and pushed it up the ramp. Soon they began removing pieces of furniture from the moving van and rolling them into the house.

Mrs. Riley greeted the Handy Helpers. "It is so nice of you to help us move. I know Beth Anne is excited that you're here."

"What would you like us to do?" Logan asked.

"My husband's car is loaded with boxes. Can you carry them into the house? They're all labeled so you'll know which room they go in."

Without another word, the guys headed for the car and began removing boxes. Most of the boxes went in the kitchen. Soon the counters were covered with boxes. Melissa noticed there was clothing hanging in Lisa Riley's minivan. "We'll take the clothes in for you," she said to Mrs. Riley.

"That would be very helpful. You can hang the clothes in the closet. Beth Anne will show you which room is hers."

Just as the girls reached the curb, they saw Beth Anne's grandmother Doris Duncan pulling up. Her car was also full of boxes.

"It looks like the gang's all here," she said with a laugh. "I should have guessed you'd be helping today."

"We'll get those boxes for you," Logan said, walking over to Doris's car.

"That's very nice of you," Doris told him. "I guess I'll go inside and help Lisa put things away."

"This is a nice room," Amber said, looking around at the freshly painted peach walls.

"Mom let me pick the color," Beth Anne said proudly, "and I helped her paint my room."

"It looks beautiful," Laura and Melissa agreed.

Soon shirts and pants were hanging in Beth Anne's closet. Melissa brought in the last of her clothes, including the dress Beth Anne's grandmother bought her to wear to church.

"Are these all of your clothes?" Melissa asked.

"Yes," Beth Anne assured her. "That's all I have."

"You have lots of nice clothes," Melissa said warmly.

The girls were ushered out of the room as the movers came in with Beth Anne's furniture. She had a twin-size bed and a dresser that had belonged to her mother when she was a child. The only new furniture in Beth Anne's room was a small desk on which she could set her computer.

Laura, Amber, and Melissa were busy bringing in Mr. and Mrs. Riley's clothes and hanging them in their closet. The guys brought in boxes that had been labeled Beth Anne's Room. Spike carried in a large plastic tote. It was difficult for him to see over the top of the tote. That was why he didn't notice the box that Chris had just brought in and placed on the floor near the door. As Spike stumbled over the box, the tote came open, and Barbie dolls, Barbie clothes, and Barbie furniture flew all over the room.

"Sorry," Spike said as he looked at the mess.

"That's okay," Beth Anne assured him. "I can pick them up by myself."

"You sure have a lot of Barbies," Spike observed, picking up one of the dolls. "Have you had these for a long time?"

"Yes, I play with them every day. They're my favorite toys."

Spike stared at the Barbies for a long moment and then asked, "Do you have an old one that you don't want anymore?"

"I like all my Barbies," Beth Anne said with a worried look on her face.

"I just asked because I need a Barbie for a project I'm working on," Spike said, hopefully. "I thought maybe if you had an old one, you could let me have it."

"I don't know," Beth Anne picked up a doll whose hair had been crushed by years of play and whose arms were marked with ink tattoos. She hugged the doll to her chest.

"Could I have that one?" Spike asked.

"I . . . I guess so." Beth Anne reluctantly handed the Barbie to Spike. "If you promise to take good care of her."

"Thanks, I promise." Spike took the doll and ran to his bike. He put the doll in his bike bag and quickly returned to help his friends carry in the remaining boxes.

The moving van was empty, and everything had been removed from the cars. Kevin Riley left for the Pizza Pan restaurant to pick up pizzas for the whole crew.

"Thanks so much for all your help," Lisa said to the Handy Helpers while everyone was enjoying their pizza.

"You're welcome, Mrs. Riley," Logan said proudly. "Helping people is what we do."

"Please call me Lisa. I'm so glad Beth Anne met you and that she can be a part of your group. That means so much to all of us."

"We're happy to have Beth Anne in the Handy Helpers," Melissa said. "She's a very good helper."

"That was nice what you said about Beth Anne," Laura told Melissa as they were getting on their bikes.

"I meant every word," Melissa assured her. "Beth Anne is sweet and fun, and I'm glad she's in our group."

"We all are," Amber added.

"I was thinking about Beth Anne's clothes, though," Melissa continued. "She doesn't have a lot of clothes, and most of her things look like she's worn them for a long time. She's smaller than we are. I have lots of outfits I've outgrown that are still really nice. Maybe I could give her some of my old clothes."

"What about your sister, Trisha?" Laura asked. "Don't you hand your clothes down to her?"

"Trisha mostly likes plain clothes like jeans and T-shirts. She hardly ever wears the clothes I give her."

"I have some clothes I can't wear anymore," Amber said, "and I don't have anybody to hand them down to."

"What about you?" Melissa asked Laura. "You must have some clothes you've outgrown."

"We have four girls in our family," Laura reminded her. "Everything gets handed down."

"But your dad is a banker," Melissa said, surprised. "He makes lots of money. He can buy you all the clothes you want."

"My dad *is* a banker, but he's all about saving money, not spending it. Both of my parents are careful with money. They call it being good stewards of God's gifts."

"Okay, well, anyway, I was thinking that we could invite Beth Anne to a sleepover at my house," Melissa went on. "We can all bring clothes that we can't wear anymore, and we can give Beth Anne a makeover."

"That sounds like a great idea!" Amber said excitedly. "When should we do it?"

"I'll have to ask my mom—I mean my parents—but I was thinking about next Friday night."

"I'll start going through my clothes. I'm sure I'll find some things that will look adorable on Beth Anne," Amber said with glee.

"I will too," Laura added, hesitantly, "but I might not have too much to contribute. Maybe I can bring some jewelry or other accessories."

"Okay, then it's a plan. I'll let you know as soon as I clear it with my parents and ask Beth Anne."

Normally, Spike would be unhappy to see Todd's Bronco parked in his driveway. But today, he was glad to see it. Everything was going according to his plan. He walked his bike around to the passenger side and quietly opened the door. From his bike bag, he took the Barbie doll he had gotten from Beth Anne. Then he reached across the back of the seat and grabbed Todd's gym bag. When Spike unzipped the gym bag, he saw a white towel inside. Pulling the towel from the bag, he quickly wrapped the Barbie doll in it. Then he replaced the towel, zipped the bag closed, and shoved it back across the seat.

Spike was about to close the passenger door when Todd came out onto the porch. Instead of slamming the door, Spike pushed it closed so it wouldn't make any noise. Unfortunately the door only partially latched. There wasn't time for him to close it again, so he left it that way. As Todd came down the walk, Spike got on his bike as if he had just been riding up.

"Hey, freak!" Todd called to him. "You'd better not scratch my Bronco with your bike!"

"How could you tell?" Spike sneered at Todd. "It has scratches all over it."

"Shut up, you little twerp!" Todd said as he got in the Bronco.

Spike watched as Todd backed out of the driveway. He must have realized a door was open. Just before he pulled into the street, he got out, walked around to the passenger side, and slammed the door. Tires squealing, Todd sped away from the curb and disappeared down the street.

CHAPTER THREE

Beth Anne opened her eyes, blinked twice, and looked around the room. It wasn't a dream. She was sleeping in her own room in their new house. She hobbled across the wooden floor to the bathroom.

Lisa was busy trying to make breakfast in a kitchen that was still piled up with boxes.

"We're just having cereal and toast," she told Beth Anne.

"I like cereal and toast," Beth Anne said, smiling. "I like our new house."

"I'll like it a lot better once everything is put away."

"Don't worry, Mom. I'll help you."

"I know you will." Lisa gave her daughter a quick squeeze. "Your dad has to work today, but we can get a lot done tomorrow."

"We can't work tomorrow!" Beth Anne sounded shocked.

"Why not?"

"Tomorrow is Sunday. We have to go to church. And tomorrow is Father's Day. We can't make Dad work on Father's Day!"

"I suppose you're right." Lisa smiled. "These boxes aren't going anywhere."

Back in her room, Beth Anne opened the tote that contained her Barbie dolls. One by one, she removed the dolls and set them out on the floor. "No Crystal," she shook her head. "I miss you, Crystal. I wonder where you are right now." Beth Anne dressed her dolls and then got dressed herself. She brushed each doll's hair before she brushed her own straight medium-blond hair. Beth Anne sat down at her desk and took out a piece of paper. At the top of the paper, she wrote "Crystal is kidnapped."

"Mom." Melissa stood at the laundry room door and watched her mother put a load of laundry in the washer.

"What is it, Melissa?"

"Could I have a sleepover next Friday?"

"That should be okay. Did you ask your dad?"

"Not yet. I wanted to ask you first."

"Will it be Amber and Laura?"

"And Beth Anne," Melissa added.

"It's very sweet that you're including Beth Anne. It will make her feel more welcome here in Bluesky."

"I know," Melissa agreed. "I was thinking that we could do something special for Beth Anne. When we helped her family move in, we noticed that she doesn't have very many nice clothes. We're going to give Beth Anne some of the clothes we've outgrown."

"That's a wonderful idea," Fran told her daughter. "How do Beth Anne and her mom feel about taking your hand-me-downs?"

"I haven't talked to them about it yet. But I'm sure Beth Anne will like it. We're going to give her a makeover."

"You'd better make sure that Beth Anne is okay with it before you go too far with your plans. You can't treat her like she's a real-life Barbie doll for you to dress up."

"It won't be like that," Melissa said, "really."

"If it's okay with your dad and with Beth Anne's mom, then you can have your sleepover."

"Can you ask Dad for me?"

"Why don't you want to ask him?"

"He'll probably say no. He doesn't want me to do anything."

"That's not true. He just wants to be a part of your life again, and he's trying to figure out where he fits into it."

"I'm not a child," Melissa said. "I'm grown-up. I can take care of myself."

"You *are* a child, just older than you were when your dad left for Afghanistan. Give him time to catch up with the changes."

Todd pulled into a parking space in front of the gym and hurried inside. As usual on a Saturday, the place was packed. Todd let out a long sigh. He wasn't going to get a quick workout in today. His friends Andy and Chase were already doing their cardio on treadmills. They waved at Todd as he headed for the men's locker room. He threw his gym bag down on the bench and unzipped it. Jennifer was going to be upset if he was late. They had plans to go to a movie. Unrolling his towel, he saw something drop from it. The man next to him saw it too.

"Aren't you a little old for dolls?" the man asked. Todd looked down to see what he was talking about. There on the floor was a Barbie doll.

"Where did that come from?" Todd asked, surprised.

"It's yours," the man said in an accusing voice. "It dropped out of your towel."

Everyone in the locker room had turned to look at Todd. "I think he came here to play Barbies," one guy said. "You're in the wrong place, buddy." That made the other men laugh. Todd quickly shoved his towel back in his bag. Picking up the doll, he tossed it in the trash and left the gym as quickly as he had entered.

"I'll get you for this, Michael!" Todd said as he got in the Bronco. "You're going to pay big-time!"

Logan looked out the front window and then looked back at the clock. Only fifteen minutes had passed since the last time he looked at the clock. His dad's plane would be landing at noon. That was still an hour away. Then it would take him at least two hours to drive up to Bluesky. Logan had mixed feelings about seeing his dad today. He was an airline pilot and had a small apartment he stayed in so he could fly out of Phoenix. It had been three weeks since his dad had come home. That time he only stayed overnight. He brought a Mother's Day gift, since he had not made it home for Mother's Day the week before. This time he planned to stay two nights. Then he would be heading back to Phoenix for a flight leaving Monday afternoon. Logan's mother, Vivian, worked at a nail salon. Monday was her day off. At least, she would be there to tell her husband good-bye before he went away for another few weeks.

Melissa finished her Saturday morning chores and asked her dad if she could go to Laura's house. He gave his permission, with instructions to be back in time to help her mother with dinner. Fran and Melissa's grandmother Sarah, who lived with them, had gone shopping. They invited Melissa to go along, but she had already spent her allowance. Shopping with no money wasn't really fun in Melissa's opinion. Her seven-year-old sister, Trisha, liked to save her allowance. So she stayed home to play air hockey with their dad.

Laura's mom, Emma, was surprised to find Melissa at their front door. "Laura isn't here. She's at Betty Jenkins's making a Father's Day cake."

"Oh . . . yeah," Melissa stammered. "I forgot about that."

"I'm sure she and Amber are still there," Emma said.

"That's okay. They're busy making their cakes. I'll talk to them later."

Melissa jumped on her bike and started to ride home. Then she changed her mind and headed in the opposite direction. Soon she was at Beth Anne's door.

"Beth Anne's in her room," Lisa said. "You know where it is. Go on in."

The door was closed, so Melissa knocked softly and called, "Beth Anne. It's me, Melissa."

Beth Anne threw open the door and invited Melissa in. "What are you doing?" Melissa asked.

"I'm organizing my Special Olympic medals," Beth Anne said sadly.

"Wow! You have a lot of medals. You must be good at Special Olympics."

"Not anymore." Beth Anne hung her head.

"Why not? Don't you want to do Special Olympics anymore?"

"I do. But there isn't any Special Olympics in Bluesky. My mom's going to find out if there's Special Olympics in Marshallville."

"Marshallville is a lot bigger than Bluesky. They probably do have Special Olympics," Melissa said encouragingly.

"I'm getting my cast off next week. Then I can be in Special Olympics swimming. I'm a good swimmer."

"Swimming! That's my best sport. I love swimming and diving. Can I join Special Olympics?"

"I think you have to be in special ed. But maybe you can be a helper. My mom can find out."

"I'm having a sleepover on Friday," Melissa said. "Would you like to come? Laura and Amber are going to be there."

"I'll ask my mom," Beth Anne said excitedly. "Let's go ask her now."

Lisa was rearranging the furniture in the living room. "A sleepover? That sounds like fun. Do you want to do that, Beth Anne?"

I'll have my cast off, and I can be with my friends," Beth Anne answered. "Please, can I?"

"I don't see why not." Lisa smiled.

"I have some clothes that don't fit me," Melissa added. "My sister, Trisha, doesn't want them. Is it okay if I give them to Beth Anne?"

"That's fine, if Beth Anne wants to take them," Lisa said. "That's very thoughtful of you."

"Do you need any help putting things away?" Melissa asked, noticing the boxes sitting around in the living room.

"Well, as a matter of fact"—Lisa looked at Beth Anne—"that's what Beth Anne was supposed to be doing this afternoon. Those boxes are full of books and things that go on the shelves over there. I'm sure she would love to have some help putting them away."

Laura was excited about their plans for the afternoon, but Amber wasn't so sure. They were headed for Betty Jenkins's house to bake Father's Day cakes. Betty was a retired mail carrier who moved to Bluesky with her husband, Paul, ten years ago. When Paul passed away, Betty stayed in Bluesky and continued as a regular at the senior center where she was the shuffleboard champ.

Amber was a little nervous about making a cake, but Laura told her not to worry. Laura was a really good cook, and everything she made turned out perfectly. Amber, on the other hand, was all thumbs when it came to cooking. She tried her best, but something always seemed to go wrong. Each girl brought a cake mix and can of frosting. Laura thought they should make the cakes from scratch, but Amber said using a mix sounded safer. Betty agreed, pointing out that they would have more time for decorating the cakes. Amber had chosen a devil's food cake mix because that was her dad's favorite. Laura brought fudge marble. She said it seemed a little fancier than plain cake. Betty already had mixing bowls and pans out so they could begin right away.

Betty showed the girls how to prepare the pan by greasing it with shortening and then sprinkling it with a light dusting of flour. Laura and Amber emptied the cake mix into mixing bowls and added eggs, water, and oil. Then they took turns using the mixer.

While the cakes were baking, they made plans for decorating the cakes. Betty showed them a picture of a cake decorated to look like a man's shirt and tie. Since both their fathers wore ties to work, they decided that would be a perfect way to decorate the cakes.

Once the cakes had cooled, they spread on the frosting. Then the fun could begin. Betty gave each girl a package of black licorice whips and showed them how to make the outline of a shirt collar and tie. As they were doing that, Betty mixed up small batches of frosting and dyed them yellow, green, and red. She scooped the colored frosting into small Ziploc bags. Then she cut a corner from each bag and showed the girls how to pipe the frosting onto the cake by squeezing the bag.

"This is fun," Amber said, surprised. "It's just like painting."

"Cake decorating is an art," Betty agreed.

"It's not that easy," Laura said in frustration. "I keep going outside the lines and my frosting isn't smooth like yours."

"Just take your time, and it will look fine," Betty encouraged Laura. "See, you're getting the hang of it."

Just as Betty said that, a large blob of red frosting landed on the white shirt, just below the tie. "Oh no," Laura groaned. "Look what I've done now!" With a spoon, she tried to scoop off the red frosting. "That's not working," Laura groaned again. "I'm just making it look worse!"

"It doesn't look that bad," Amber assured her. "No one will even notice."

Once the colored frosting had been applied as the background for the tie, each girl selected candies to complete the tie design. At last, they stood back and admired their work.

"Yours looks a lot better than mine," Laura admitted. "My tie is crooked, and it looks like ketchup spilled all over the shirt." Laura indicated the additional red blotches of frosting that hadn't landed where she planned.

"I'm sure your dad will like it anyway," Amber said. "This was a lot of fun, Betty. Thanks for letting us use your kitchen."

"It was fun for me too." Betty smiled. "Both of your cakes look lovely. I'm sure your dads will be thrilled."

Just as they were finishing the cleanup, Laura's mom rang the doorbell. "Would you like a ride home?" she offered Amber.

"That might be a good idea," Amber said. "I planned to walk home, but I wouldn't want anything to happen to this cake. Decorating it was a lot of work!"

"Well, your cakes look great," Emma told the girls. "That will be a nice surprise for your dads."

Spike was just about finished sweeping the front porch and sidewalk after mowing the lawn. When Spike saw Todd and Jennifer pull up in the driveway, he was hoping Todd would stay in the car, but no such luck. "That's all I need," Spike said under his breath. Jennifer said good-bye at the front door, and Todd came back down the sidewalk.

"Are you missing any of your Barbie dolls?" Todd asked sarcastically. Spike looked at him as if he didn't know what Todd was talking about. "I just ask 'cause I found one in my gym bag. I'm pretty sure it's yours."

Spike shrugged his shoulders and went back to sweeping.

"Keep your hands off my stuff, you weirdo!" Todd shouted back at Spike as he got in his Bronco and sped away.

CHAPTER FOUR

As Logan came into the living room, he saw his dad remove the sheets from the sofa and fold them. Logan shook his head, realizing his dad had slept on the sofa.

"Happy Father's Day." Logan attempted a smile. "Here, I got you this."

Carl Green tore through the wrappings to find a framed picture. It was Logan and his mother Vivian seated on a bench in the park. His mother was smiling but had a sort of sad, faraway look on her face. Logan was sitting up straight as if he were posing for a formal photo in a studio.

Carl thanked his son for the picture, placing it on his suitcase. Then he opened the card Logan had just handed him. The caption on the front of the card read, "What is a Father?" Inside, the card described the ideal father who worked hard but found time to spend with his children.

"I thought we could go to Pine Lake today," Carl told his son. "We can rent a boat and go fishing. I know you and your mom like to fish."

"That's fine," Logan said, quietly.

Vivian Green was fully dressed when she came into the living room to greet her husband and son. Normally, on a Sunday morning, she would stay in her pajamas and slippers until after breakfast.

"I'll make us something to eat," she said, heading for the kitchen.

Everyone was quiet as they ate their breakfast of eggs, bacon, and toast. "Logan thinks going fishing sounds like a good idea," Carl said to his wife as she removed the dirty dishes from the table. "What do you think?"

"That sounds fine with me. I'll pack us a picnic lunch while you two get everything ready."

"It looks like a lot of other people had the same idea," Carl said as he parked the car in the crowded parking lot at Pine Lake. The lake was already dotted with sailboats, kayaks, and canoes, as well as fishing boats. After talking with the man running the boat rental, Carl returned to the car where his wife and son were waiting.

"All they have left are two-man canoes," he said, disappointed.

"That's okay," Vivian tried to smile. "You and Logan take the boat out. It'll give you a chance to be together. I'll take a hike around the lake."

"Couldn't we try to fit three people in the boat?" Logan pleaded.

"The man at the rental place said we can't," Carl assured him. "We could take turns, I guess."

"No, you two go," Vivian said again. "After my hike, I'll get lunch ready."

Logan and Carl loaded their fishing gear into the canoe and paddled out onto the lake. The pebbled bottom along the shoreline soon disappeared. The water became smooth and deep. Tall pine trees surrounded the lake on all sides. Passing some boats that were stopped on the water, Carl and Logan waved to people already fishing. Logan was seated in the front, with his dad in the rear. Carl steered the boat toward an inlet they had fished in many times. It was a small cove lined with huge boulders and small scrubby bushes. They stopped paddling and let the canoe coast to a stop.

"This looks like a good spot," Carl said.

"Yeah," Logan agreed without turning around. "I think we caught a couple of good-sized bass here last year."

They readied their lines and cast them into the water. Then came the long wait for a bite. Logan felt relieved that fishing was a sport that required quiet. He wasn't sure what to say to his dad. It had been so long since they'd spent any time together.

"Are you having a nice summer so far?" Carl asked after a long silence.

"Pretty good," Logan answered.

"What have you been doing?"

"I went fishing at Fox Creek with Chris and helped some people move into their house."

"Do you have any plans?"

"Not really."

After their brief conversation, the silence returned. Logan looked out at the ducks on the lake. "Dabblers and divers," he said mostly to himself.

"You remember!" Carl said, sitting up in the canoe. "That was at least a year ago that I told you about the ducks."

"Sure." Logan smiled a little. "The dabblers stick their heads in the water to look for food. The divers go all the way under water to catch small fish."

"What's the other way you can tell them apart?"

"Divers have big feet, and dabblers have small feet."

"Very good," Carl praised his son. "Do you know the names of any of the ducks?"

"Those are mallards over there, I'm pretty sure," Logan said after glancing around the lake and pointing at some ducks with dark-green heads and bright-yellow bills.

"They are. What about that one?" Carl pointed toward a duck with a chestnut-colored breast. It had white cheeks and what looked like a black cap on his head.

"I'm not sure," Logan said thoughtfully. "Maybe it's a ruddy duck."

"Exactly. Dabbler or diver?"

"Diver, I think."

"Correct again. What about over there?" This time Carl pointed toward some ducks that were dark gray with bright-white bills.

"I don't remember," Logan admitted.

"Those are American coot," Carl told him. "And they're divers too."

"What about those over—?" Logan didn't have a chance to finish his sentence before his dad silenced him.

"Look over there," Carl said in a whisper.

Logan followed his father's finger until he spotted a blue heron behind a large rock near the water's edge. Its long neck and bill were barely visible against the rocks. As they watched, the heron turned its head to look at them. Very carefully, Carl removed his cell phone from his pocket and took pictures of the blue heron. The two in the boat sat perfectly still and watched as the heron jumped from rock to rock. After observing it for some time, Carl looked at his watch. He whispered Logan's name and pointed to his oar. Gliding as quietly as possible, they rowed the boat out of the cove. As if he were saying good-bye to old friends, the heron ran along the shore in their direction until the boat was out in open waters.

"That was really something!" Logan gasped once he felt it was safe to talk.

"I've never seen anything like it!" Carl shook his head in amazement.

"You won't believe what we saw!" Logan ran toward his mother, who was unpacking the picnic basket.

"What did you see?" Vivian asked her excited son.

"It was a blue heron. Show her the pictures, Dad!"

Carl took out his phone and held it out for Vivian.

"This guy's a duck expert," Carl said proudly. "He pretty much knew the names of all the ducks on the lake."

"Not really," Logan said shyly. "But I did remember some of them."

"Did you catch any fish?" Vivian asked.

"Not today," Carl said, "but we did see a guy pull a big trout out of the lake."

"We should go bird-watching again," Carl suggested once they were home. "I'll be back in a few weeks. Would you like to do that?"

"Can I bring a friend?" Logan asked.

"Sure. Would that be Chris or Spike?"

"Neither." Logan looked away. "I was thinking of someone else—someone who really likes birds too."

Melissa was on her way to the kitchen with plans to make breakfast for her family. It would be a Father's Day surprise. Last year her dad had been stationed in Afghanistan. They wished him happy Father's Day on Skype. He told them he had limp bacon and runny eggs for breakfast. Melissa promised that when he was home, she would make him some of her famous pancakes.

As Melissa passed her parents' bedroom, she noticed her sister, Trisha, crouched in front of the door, holding a present between her knees. "Come on and help me with breakfast," she whispered. "Let Mom and Dad sleep as long as they can."

In the kitchen, Melissa poured the ingredients for buttermilk pancakes into a bowl and handed Trisha a spoon. "Mix this up while I cook the bacon. I'm going to make it nice and crisp, just the way Dad likes it."

As she watched the bacon sizzling in the pan, Melissa thought about how much their lives had changed in the two weeks since her dad had been home. At first, she was really excited about doing lots of things with him. But sometimes her dad was in a bad mood and just wanted to lie in the hammock in the backyard. Other times, he wanted to know everything she was doing. He expected her to ask permission to do things her mom always let her do—things like talking on the phone or fixing a snack.

"He's just trying to figure out what his role is in our family," her mother had told her. "Give it time, and everything will work itself out."

Melissa was trying to be patient, but she wondered if things were ever going to get better. "Good morning," she said as her dad came into the kitchen. "Happy Father's Day."

"It sure smells good in here." Cody looked at both his daughters working together. "Looks like you two have everything under control."

"Happy Father's Day, Daddy." Trisha ran to him and put her arms around his waist. Cody bent down and kissed the top of his young daughter's head.

"It's sure nice to be spending Father's Day at home with my girls."

"Breakfast's almost ready," Melissa announced. "Better get Mom and Grandma," she said to Trisha.

"Change your clothes," Emma told her daughters as soon as they arrived home from church. "We're supposed to be at the Smiths' at one o'clock."

"You're not taking that cake!" Laura exclaimed as she looked at the food her mother packed to take to the Smiths'. There in the back of the Suburban—among her mother's superbly delicious red beans and rice, pecan pie, and pralines—sat Laura's not-so-nice-looking Father's Day cake.

"Of course we're taking it," Emma said matter-of-factly. "Why wouldn't we?"

"It just doesn't look as good as I was hoping."

"I'm sure it will taste great. That's all that matters."

Laura squeezed into the backseat along with the folding chairs her father had placed there. Her three sisters were already seat-belted into the middle seats, leaving her no choice. It was only a ten-minute ride to the Smiths', but Laura dreaded every minute.

As the Thomases pulled up in front of the Smith house, they saw Spike sitting in the front-porch glider. He had his head down and was scraping his feet across the cement. He looked up as they pulled into the driveway.

"Hi!" Spike waved in their direction.

"How about giving us a hand?" Bill yelled as he opened the clam doors on the back of the Suburban.

"Sure." Spike came down the steps two at a time.

"Here." Emma handed him Laura's Father's Day cake.

"Who made this?" Spike asked, looking curiously at the cake in his hands.

"Laura did," Emma told him.

Spike carried the cake into the house. Todd and Jennifer came out the front door to help Bill with the chairs he was taking out of the Suburban.

"Who murdered your cake?" Spike asked Laura as he set the cake on the dessert table.

"Nobody," Laura said, surprised. "It's supposed to be a shirt and tie."

"Yeah," Spike commented, "with a bullet hole in it!"

"I had a little trouble with the frosting, that's all."

"That's a relief!" Spike sighed loudly.

"What do you mean?" Laura asked.

"That's frosting, not blood." Spike pointed to the red stains on the cake.

"Everyone's in the backyard." Carolyn directed the Thomases through the kitchen toward the sliding door.

Her husband, David, was standing near the grill. "Glad you're here." He extended his hand to Bill, who accepted his handshake.

Carolyn and Emma returned to the kitchen to finish up some last-minute preparations. Their husbands continued their conversation while David got the grill ready.

"Want to play with Tigger?" Monica asked as Laura's two younger sisters, Molly and Taylor, came running toward her. Monica was holding a pure-white miniature Siberian husky. It was her sister Jennifer's dog, but Monica and Spike spent more time playing with her than Jennifer did.

"Yippee!" Four-year-old Taylor jumped up and down.

"Can she do any tricks?" asked her six-year-old sister, Molly.

"She can do lots of tricks. Just watch." With that, Monica placed Tigger on the grass and began issuing commands to sit, beg, roll over, and play dead.

"She's a smart dog!" Molly said in amazement.

"She is a smart dog!" Taylor echoed.

Molly gave Taylor a dirty look.

"I didn't mean to copy you," Taylor said with her head down.

Monica left the dog in the care of the two young girls and joined the other teenagers who were seated around the table. Jennifer and Todd were sitting together in one lawn chair, his arm around her waist. Mandy, Laura's older sister, was seated in a chair nearby. Mandy looked with envy at the shorts and tops Monica and Jennifer were wearing. Her mother would never let her wear something that short. Mandy tried telling her mom that her ballet costumes were more revealing than shorts, but her mom said it wasn't the same thing. Monica and Mandy were both going into tenth grade in the fall. While they were friendly to each other, they weren't really friends. Monica was into sports, especially softball. Mandy had been studying ballet since she could walk. Mandy usually had her nose stuck in a book—romance was her favorite. Monica preferred movies, especially action films.

Carolyn called to Jennifer to come and help her in the kitchen. When Jennifer got up, Todd followed her into the house.

"How's your summer going?" Monica asked Mandy.

"Okay, I guess. I've been helping my mom at her dance studio."

"That sounds like fun," Monica said with a smile.

"It might be, except I already have three younger sisters to take care of. Trying to get somebody else's little girls to do what I say isn't that much fun."

"I know what you mean." Monica sighed. "I've been babysitting for this lady who has a two-year-old and a four-year-old—both girls. They can really be a handful. I don't remember being so bossy when I was four!"

"At least, you get paid." Mandy sighed. "I'm just expected to pitch in and help my mom."

"That's a bummer," Monica agreed.

"Does Jennifer have a job?" Mandy asked.

"She's working part-time at the Pizza Pan."

"Doesn't Todd work there too?"

"That's where they met."

"Do you think they're serious?" Mandy looked at Monica.

"Naw, Jennifer only goes with a guy for three months. Todd's time is almost up. Besides, she'd never marry someone named Jensen."

"Why not?"

"Her name would be Jennifer Jensen."

"Maybe everybody would call her Jen-Jen," Mandy said in a sing-song voice.

"She'd love that. Hey, Jen-Jen!" Monica called to her sister as she came through the sliding glass door, Todd close on her heels.

"Why'd you call me that?" Jennifer looked curiously at her sister.

"Jennifer Jensen," Monica laughed, "get it?"

"Oh, shut up!" Jennifer turned and went back in the house.

Todd, who remained in the backyard, turned his attention to Spike, who had been giving the little girls some advice about how to get the dog to do tricks.

"Want to play some one-on-one basketball?" Todd asked Spike.

"I'm kinda tired." Spike plopped down on one of the lawn chairs on the patio.

"Go ahead," his dad urged. "That was nice of Todd to offer. It'll be fun."

"Sure it will," Spike muttered under his breath, "about as much fun as having your tonsils out."

"What was that? I didn't hear you," Todd grabbed the ball and walked toward Spike.

"I said, 'It'll be fun taking you out.'"

"Oh, you think so?" Todd laughed. "We'll have to see about that!"

Laura had remained in the kitchen with her mother and Carolyn, hoping they would give her something to do. Also, she wanted to stay far away from the dessert table where her cake was certain to draw more comments. When Spike and Todd came through the house on their way to the driveway, Laura followed them.

"You wanna play?" Todd directed his question at Laura, who shook her head no. "How about a game of horse? We can play to see who does the dishes."

"We're eating on paper plates," Spike pointed out. "There won't be any dishes."

"I meant the dishes at *my* house," Todd said with a creepy laugh.

Spike dribbled the ball as he walked to the first mark. After a few seconds, he took his shot. A wave of relief came over Spike as he watched the ball swish into the net. With his next shot, he wasn't so lucky. The ball hit the rim and bounced back. Todd caught it and dribbled to the beginning mark. His first three shots went in. When his fourth shot missed, he passed the ball to Spike, a little bit harder than he needed to. But Spike was able to catch it without showing any surprise.

The game continued until Todd only had one shot left. It was an easy shot, and Spike was sure he missed it on purpose. Spike missed his shot from the free-throw line, and Todd won with the next shot.

"Good game." Todd tossed the ball to Spike and headed for the front door. "Guess you'll be doing the dishes," he called over his shoulder.

"Todd seems nice," Laura said as Spike bounced the ball against the side of the garage.

"That's because you're here." Spike slammed the ball hard on the ground so that it bounced straight up in the air.

"You don't like him?" Laura questioned further.

"Not a two-faced jerk like that!"

"Why do you call him two-faced?"

"He's real nice when Jennifer's with him, saying I'm his bro or his buddy. But when no one's around, he calls me names like dummy or jerk-face and punches me a lot."

"Why don't you tell your parents?"

"I've tried. Todd has two older brothers. My mom thinks he's just treating me like a younger brother—you know—the way his brothers treat him."

"What do you think? Is he just treating you like a brother?"

"I don't wanna be his brother. I just want him to leave me alone!"

"Do you think Jennifer is serious about him?"

"Naw, she'll break up with him soon, and that'll be the end of Todd."

CHAPTER FIVE

"Don't make any plans for this morning," Carolyn told her son. "You have some shopping to do."

"Shopping?" Spike looked at his mother as if she was crazy. "Yesterday was Father's Day, and there aren't any birthdays this month. Why do I have to go shopping?"

"You're going to use some of your allowance to buy a new Barbie doll for Beth Anne."

"I didn't take Beth Anne's doll. She gave it to me."

"You still shouldn't have taken it."

"I can't believe Todd ratted me out," Spike said, mostly to himself.

"Todd didn't *rat* you out," Carolyn informed him. "Jennifer told me. Laura was with us in the kitchen. She said that Beth Anne's Barbies are her favorite toys. She treats them like they're real people. Taking her doll was wrong, not to mention putting it in Todd's gym bag. I can't think of any reason you would do that."

"It was just a gag. That's all. I thought Todd would think it was funny."

"Well, it was embarrassing! You wouldn't like it if he did that to you!"

"Guess not. I'll tell him I'm sorry. I'll tell Beth Anne I'm sorry too."

"That's a good idea, but you still have to replace her doll."

Carolyn pulled into a parking space at the Walmart in Marshallville. She led the way to the toy department and indicated a long aisle filled with Barbie dolls and Barbie gear. "Here you are," she said.

"I can't go down that aisle." Spike turned his head away. "It's too pink."

"What does that matter?" Carolyn asked. "Just find a doll for Beth Anne. I'll meet you at the checkout."

"I can't go down that aisle!" Spike said more forcefully as his mother walked away. "That much pink will make me puke!"

Spike focused on his feet as he shuffled down the aisle. Two little girls wearing pink shorts and Barbie shirts were admiring the castle at the end of the aisle. They stared curiously as Spike came toward them. He looked up just long enough to check the prices. Spike wanted to buy a doll wearing more clothes, but the cheapest ones were wearing swimsuits. With one sweep of his arm, he lifted a box with a Barbie clothed in a flowered pink-and-orange two-piece swimsuit.

With his mission accomplished, Spike knew he had a little time left before his mom would finish her shopping. He was thinking about checking out the soaker guns when he heard a noise coming from the next aisle. *Pfffbt! Pfffbt! Pffbt! Somebody's got a real gas problem,* Spike thought. Poking his head around the corner, he saw a girl and boy about six or seven years old. They were bouncing up and down on whoopee cushions, producing the farting sounds he heard. Just as Spike was coming their way, their mother yelled at them from the other end of the aisle. Quick as a wink, they put the whoopee cushions back and ran to their mother's cart.

I wonder what happened to the whoopee cushion I used to have? Spike thought. *I bet Mom found it. Maybe I should get another one. You never know when it can come in handy.*

Spike quickly picked out a red-colored whoopee cushion and headed for the checkout counter. He would have to be fast. If his mom saw him with the whoopee cushion, she'd never let him buy it. He was standing near the door when his mother finished her shopping.

"Did you find a nice doll for Beth Anne?" she asked.

"Sure did." Spike removed the doll from the bag and showed her. "She'll really like this one."

"How about some lunch?" Carolyn suggested when they were back in the car.

"Sure. Where're we going?"

"I was thinking about the Pizza Pan. Is that okay?"

"I . . . guess . . . so," Spike groaned.

"You don't want to have pizza for lunch?" Carolyn asked.

"It's not that," Spike hesitated.

"It's because Todd works there," Carolyn said. "Is that it?"

"Well . . ."

"You said you wanted to apologize. This'll give you a chance to tell him you're sorry."

The Pizza Pan restaurant was filled with the usual lunch crowd. It was a popular place in Bluesky because of the weekday buffet. There were lots of pizza choices as well as pastas and salads. Spike loaded his plate with pieces of sausage, pepperoni, and bacon pizza. "How about some salad?" his mother suggested. "I'd like to see some green on your plate."

Carolyn returned to their table, and Spike grabbed a bowl to get some salad. "Look here. It's the Barbie-napper!" Spike looked up to see Todd placing some fresh pizzas on the buffet.

"Leave me alone!" Spike shot a dirty look at Todd.

"You're safe for now, you little crybaby, but just wait—oh, hi, Mrs. Smith." Spike turned around to see his mother walking back toward the buffet. "I was just telling Michael that Friday is my day off. I thought we might spend some time together and get to know each other better."

"That's very nice of you," Carolyn smiled at Todd. "What do you think, Michael? Wouldn't you like to have some fun with Todd?"

"I . . . I . . . m-m-might be busy on Friday," Spike sputtered. "But thanks anyway."

"Very funny." Carolyn gave Spike a stern look. "He's not busy on Friday. I'm sure he would enjoy spending time with you."

"Then it's all set," Todd said. "I'll pick you up about nine o'clock."

"That was nice of Todd, wasn't it?" Carolyn asked Spike once they were back at their table.

"Yeah, real nice," Spike said sarcastically. "I can hardly wait 'til Friday."

"You're around women all the time at home. Spending time with Todd will be good for you. You need a role model."

"Why does it have to be Todd?"

"He's respectful toward Jennifer, goes to church, and doesn't have any bad habits," Carolyn replied.

"You mean like smoking or drinking or drugs?"

"That's exactly what I mean. He has a job, and he has plans to go to college. He's a very respectable young man. Just give him a chance. That's all your dad and I are asking you to do. Do you think you can do that?"

"I'll try," Spike said, reluctantly.

Beth Anne was wishing she had her cast off so she could ride her bike to the senior center for the Handy Helper meeting Monday afternoon. At least, this was the last week with that bulky thing on her leg. And she was glad that her mom was willing to drive her there and pick her up after the meeting.

Lisa Riley parked the minivan in front of the big cream-colored building with green trim. She helped Beth Anne out of the backseat and walked slowly with her into the senior center. As usual, Gus Farley, one of the original organizers of the senior center, was seated in the recreation room with some of his friends. As he always did in the summer, Gus was wearing Bermuda shorts and a Hawaiian shirt. His bald head was covered with a baseball cap.

"Hey there, Beth Anne," Gus called out when he saw them. "When are you getting that thing off your leg?"

"On Wednesday." Beth Anne and her mother walked over to where the men were sitting.

"Bet you can't wait for that," Gus said with a laugh.

"That's for sure." Beth Anne sighed. "It seems like I've had this cast forever!"

"You remember Bert and Norman, don't you?" Gus waved his arm in the direction of his two friends. They were dressed in shorts and T-shirts. Bert was wearing white socks and hiking boots.

"Of course I do," Beth Anne said. "But where's Al?"

"He's visiting his grandkids in Seattle for the summer," Norman spoke up. "He'll be back in September."

"Got any broken-leg jokes for her, Gus?" Bert asked his friend.

"Well . . ." Gus thought for a moment. "It's not exactly a broken-leg joke, but what goes ninety-nine thump, ninety-nine thump, ninety-nine thump?"

"I don't know," Beth Anne admitted.

"It's a centipede with a wooden leg."

"That's funny, Gus." Beth Anne laughed. "I have a joke for you. What do you call a grandfather clock?"

"That's a tough one." Gus shook his head. "What is it?"

"It's an old timer—like you!" Beth Anne pointed her finger at Gus.

"Well played." Norman held up a hand to give Beth Anne a high five.

"I wouldn't laugh if I were you." Gus turned to his friend. "You're an old timer too, you know."

Just then, the rest of the Handy Helpers came through the front door of the senior center.

"Gotta go." Beth Anne waved to Gus and his friends. "See you later, alligator."

"After a while, crocodile." The three seniors waved back.

There were seven members of the Handy Helpers. Every Monday, they met at the senior center to find out what jobs they had been assigned by the volunteer coordinator, Mrs. Snow. Chris, Logan, and Spike were the original junior volunteers. They called themselves Three Handy Guys. When Amber, Laura, and Melissa wanted to be volunteers too, the guys weren't exactly thrilled. In fact, when the girls started calling themselves the Happy Helpers, it seemed like they were trying to take over. After fighting against each other and getting into some trouble with Walt, the director, the two groups decided to join forces. That's how they became the Handy Helpers.

When Beth Anne came to Bluesky to live with her grandmother Doris Duncan, she wanted to be a Handy Helper too. Some of the members were okay with that idea, but Logan and Melissa were afraid that Beth Anne might not be able to do the work because she has Down syndrome. After Beth Anne risked her life trying to find Cher, the toy poodle the Andersons left in the care of the Handy Helpers, everyone agreed she should be allowed to join. That's how Beth Anne became the seventh member of the Handy Helpers.

"Hi, everyone," Walt greeted them as they sat down at the table in the copy room. "How's your summer going so far?"

"Fine," they all assured him. "But it always goes by too fast," Melissa added.

"Wait until you're my age." Walt laughed. "Then you'll see how fast time really flies."

"At least, we have more time to help out here," Logan said. "But I didn't see any jobs on the assignment sheet."

"Mrs. Snow didn't put you on it because she has something different in mind for you to help with, and she wanted to make sure it would be okay."

"Of course," Laura said excitedly. "We always like to do different jobs around here."

"Well," Walt explained, "this is not a job you'll be doing around here. It's more of a job you'll do around town. You may have noticed the peach trees in lots of backyards—including plenty of the seniors'. The peaches are just getting ripe. It's hard for some of the seniors to pick the peaches, so we do that for them. They keep the peaches they want, and we donate some to the food bank. Some of the peaches end up back here, and we have a group of ladies who turn the peaches into jam."

"Picking peaches sounds like fun," Amber said.

"Sure," Logan added. "We can climb the trees and hand the peaches down to the girls."

"Maybe we can do the tree climbing and hand the peaches down to you guys," Amber shot back.

"We have plenty of ladders." Walt laughed. "There won't be any tree-climbing involved."

"When will you be doing this?" Chris asked.

"On Thursday," Walt said. "We usually meet here at about eight o'clock in the morning."

"Sorry," Chris told him. "I won't be able to help. My brother Eric and I are flying to California on Wednesday. We'll be spending a week with our grandparents."

"That sounds like more fun than picking peaches," Melissa said.

"Yeah, my grandparents live near the beach, and they promised to take us to Disneyland."

"Disneyland?" Beth Anne perked up. "I want to go to Disneyland!"

"I guess you can count on the rest of us." Logan looked around as everyone shook their heads yes.

"I'm getting my cast off on Wednesday," Beth Anne announced, "so I can help too."

"Of course." Walt smiled. "We need all the help we can get."

Just as the meeting was coming to an end, Lisa Riley stuck her head in the door and asked if Beth Anne was ready to go. "Chris is going to Disneyland," Beth Anne said. "I want to go to Disneyland."

"Maybe you will someday." Lisa hugged her daughter. "But we just moved in a new house and started new jobs. It'll be awhile before we can take a vacation."

"I've gotta go too," Spike said as Beth Anne hobbled out the door. "See you Thursday."

"He sure was quiet," Melissa observed after Spike left. "I wonder what's bugging him."

"Yeah," Amber agreed. "He didn't even make a comment when I said that girls can climb trees."

"His parents are keeping him pretty busy at home," Chris told them. "He couldn't even go fishing with us."

"I think there's more to it," Laura said seriously. "He's having trouble with his sister's boyfriend, Todd. Spike told me that Todd picks on him when no one's watching. He's really been giving him a hard time."

"Why doesn't he tell his parents?" Chris asked.

"I guess he's tried," Laura explained. "But his parents think he's exaggerating and that Todd is just trying to be like a big brother."

"I'll see if there's anything I can do to help," Logan suggested.

"Don't tell him I said anything," Laura added. "He might not like us talking about him."

"I won't," Logan promised. "I'll be cool."

Beth Anne and Lisa had just gotten into the house when there was a knock on the door. Lisa opened it to find Spike standing there. "Can I talk to Beth Anne for a minute?" Spike asked.

"Sure," Lisa said. "She just went in her room. Is anything wrong?"

"No," Spike assured her. "I have something to give Beth Anne."

Beth Anne was turning on her computer when Spike came into her room. "Hi there," he said.

"Oh!" Beth Anne gasped. "I didn't see you."

"Sorry if I scared you. Your mom said it was okay."

"Are you going to take another Barbie?" Beth Anne asked, concerned.

"No, I have a Barbie doll for *you*—to replace the one I took." Spike handed her the box with the new Barbie.

"This is for me?" Beth Anne asked, cheering up. "She can be New Crystal!" Beth Anne tore open the package and took out the doll, hugging it tightly to herself. "Look," she said to the Barbie dolls sitting in a line on her bed, "this is New Crystal."

As if she had forgotten that Spike was there, Beth Anne knelt down in front of her dolls. "New Crystal will be your new friend. I don't know where Old Crystal is, but I know she's safe. I asked God to take care of her. He will keep her safe."

Spike pictured Old Crystal lying on a heap of trash at the town dump. He didn't have the heart to tell Beth Anne the truth. As Beth Anne continued to have a one-sided conversation with her dolls, Spike walked over to her desk to look at her computer. Next to the computer he saw a piece of notebook paper. His eyes were drawn to it when he noticed the title written on the paper, "Crystal is Kidnapped." Trying not to be obvious, Spike began to read Beth Anne's story:

One minute I had my Crystal with me, until somebody took her away from me. Suddenly I went to my parents to let them know what happened to my Crystal. So they put up a flier so somebody would find my Crystal. One day my wish came true when a boy saw the flyer and he went to find my Crystal. Even though my Crystal had been kidnapped, suddenly the boy found my Crystal and brought her back to me. The End.

"See you later," Spike called out as he left Beth Anne's room.

"You forgot to say *alligator*," Beth Anne called after him, but he was already gone.

Spike could feel the tears well up in his eyes. He quickly wiped them away with his sleeve and hurried to his bike. He hadn't realized how much Beth Anne loved her Barbies. He felt guilty knowing that he had broken his promise to take good care of Crystal. He could never tell Beth Anne the truth about the final fate of her beloved doll. And he felt anger toward Todd for driving him to the point where he would do something like that. More than that, he was angry with himself for letting Todd get to him. *Whatever happens next*, Spike thought, *it's between me and Todd.*

Chris stowed his bag in the overhead compartment and took his seat on the plane next to his brother Eric. The flight from Phoenix to Los Angeles, California, was less than an hour. His grandparents would be there eagerly awaiting their arrival. Chris was thinking about the cool breezes that blew in from the ocean and the smell of oranges coming from the trees in their backyard. Spending time with their father's parents was always special. It was the best way he knew to get to know his dad.

Eric and Chris lost their father to a car accident over seven years before. Eric was five at the time, and Chris was not quite three. Eric remembered his dad teaching him to ride a bike and throw a ball. Chris tried to remember his dad, but he knew his memories were based on pictures he had seen, not real memories. Everyone said that Chris looked just like his dad and that he was like him in other ways too. He was easygoing and fun, just as his dad had been.

Maintaining a relationship with their father's family was important to their mother, Joyce. She insisted that they write letters or call on the phone. She sent their grandparents pictures and invited them to come for visits. After she remarried, she felt even more determined to keep in touch. Mason Fuller was a good father to Eric and Chris. He spent lots of time with them and helped with things like Boy Scout campouts and sports activities. Eric and Chris both called him Dad. After their baby brother, Tyler, was born, the family seemed complete.

As soon as Chris and Eric exited the plane, they saw their grandparents waving excitedly. Grandpa Sam was tall with a healthy tan. His salt-and-pepper hair had more gray than the last time they had seen him, but otherwise, he seemed unchanged. He had recently retired as an executive with a small computer firm. Their grandmother Maureen was a tiny woman with dark-blond hair and expressive blue eyes. Her face lit up when she saw the boys. She liked to describe herself as someone who never grew up. Eric and Chris knew they were always in for fun times with Grandma Mo.

Beth Anne was fidgeting in her seat at the doctor's office waiting room. It seemed like they had been there for hours. Finally she heard her name being called. "I'm hobbling in," she told Yolanda, the nurse, "but I'm skipping out."

Yolanda just smiled. "Well, let's wait and see."

"Hi there, Beth Anne," Dr. O'Connor said as he entered the examination room. "How's your leg feeling?"

"Itchy." Beth Anne frowned.

"Well, we should be able to get that thing off today. Then you can wash your leg and put on some lotion. That should help with the itching. First, though, we need an x-ray to make sure everything is healed the way we want it."

Beth Anne was helped down the hallway by Yolanda, who assisted her as she got up on the x-ray table. When the x-ray technician finished taking pictures of her leg, Beth Anne returned to wait with her mother for the results.

"Everything looks good," Dr. O'Connor told them. "You're going to get your cast off today. What do you think about that?"

"I think I'm happy about that!" Beth Anne clapped her hands. But her joy turned to fear when she saw what was in Dr. O'Connor's hand. It was a saw.

"You won't cut my leg off by accident?" Beth Anne said, frightened.

"Oh no," Dr. O'Connor laughed. "This saw cuts casts. It doesn't cut skin. It just vibrates, see." Dr. O'Connor gave a demonstration with the saw.

"It might tickle a little," Nurse Yolanda added, "but it won't hurt you."

Once the cast was removed, Beth Anne stared in shock at her leg. It was pasty white and covered with flaky, dead skin. It looked smaller than her other leg.

"It smells rotten!" Beth Anne wrinkled her nose.

"Well, it hasn't been washed in six weeks." Dr. O'Connor laughed. He checked her leg for sores. Then he took it in his hands and moved it around. "Everything seems to be in good shape, but you'll have to take it easy for a while."

"What restrictions will she have?" Lisa asked the doctor.

"Well, no strenuous activities or sports."

"Can I ride my bike?" Beth Anne asked.

"I'd hold off on that until after your follow-up visit in a few weeks."

"What about swimming?" Lisa asked.

"Swimming should be okay if she doesn't overdo it. In fact, swimming would be good exercise."

Dr. O'Connor gave Lisa a sheet of paper with instructions. "This should tell you what you need to know, but if you have any questions, please call."

Beth Anne stood up, preparing to leave. "Oh, that hurts," she said, putting weight on her leg for the first time.

"I don't think she'll be doing any skipping." Lisa laughed.

"Maybe on your next visit," Yolanda told Beth Anne.

"I can still pick peaches tomorrow," Beth Anne announced once they were in the car.

"Beth Anne, you heard what the doctor said. You've got to take it easy."

"I'll be careful. I promise."

"Maybe they can find an easy job for you to do. But no climbing on ladders."

"Mom, you missed our street!" Beth Ann called out as her mother continued down the main road from the doctor's office.

"We're going to make one stop on our way home," Lisa said. "If it works out, you'll be very happy."

Lisa pulled into a small parking lot in front of a tiny white wood-frame building.

"What is this place?" Beth Anne asked.

"It's the Chamber of Commerce. I thought if anyone knows if there is Special Olympics in Bluesky, it would be the people here."

As Beth Anne and Lisa came through the door, they were greeted by Susie, a perky young woman with wavy blond hair and sparkling brown eyes. "How are you today?" she asked with a friendly smile.

"I just got my cast off," Beth Anne told her. "Doesn't my leg look funny?"

"Congratulations," Susie said, studying Beth Anne's outstretched leg.

"We're here to find out about Special Olympics," Lisa told Susie. "Do you know if there is a group in Bluesky?"

"I'm not sure, but Mr. Dugan over there might know. He's the president of the Chamber of Commerce." Susie pointed in the direction of three men who were having a jovial conversation in the corner. "Mr. Dugan!" Susie called out, "These people would like to talk to you."

The three men looked in the direction of Lisa and Beth Anne. Quickly, one man walked toward them. He was dressed in tan slacks and a light-blue shirt. "Hello, I'm Emmitt Dugan, and I think I know who you are. Aren't you Beth Anne?"

"How do you know?" Beth Anne asked, surprised.

"You're kind of famous in Bluesky," Mr. Dugan said with a wide grin. "You've been on the news quite a bit lately, first for saving that little girl at the lake and then for your rescue from Harper's Hill."

"I know," Beth Anne said, "but that's all over with. Now I want to be in Special Olympics."

"Hi, I'm Lisa Riley, Beth Anne's mother. We came here to find out if there is a Special Olympics group in Bluesky."

"I know there's one in Marshallville," Mr. Dugan said thoughtfully, "but I don't think we have one in Bluesky."

"I guess we'll have to go to Marshallville then," Lisa said sadly. "Beth Anne really wants to be in Special Olympics swimming."

"Go to Marshallville?" The other two men came walking toward them. One man was short with a jiggly belly that hung over his dark-gray belted dress pants. His light-brown hair was cut short and stuck up a little in the back. "Why would you want to go to Marshallville? We have everything you need here in Bluesky."

"This is Mayor Goodwin," Mr. Dugan said, stepping aside as the mayor joined the group.

"And this is my right-hand man, Troy Fillmore." Mayor Goodwin indicated the tall, slim black man who was at his side. "He's our town manager."

"Hello there," Mr. Fillmore extended his hand to Lisa. "I feel like I know you both. My wife is with the police department."

"Of course," Lisa said. "She stayed with us while everyone was looking for Beth Anne. She's a very kind woman."

"Yes, she is." Mr. Fillmore smiled. "Is there anything we can help you with?"

"We came here to find out if there is a Special Olympics group in Bluesky, but I guess we'll have to join the group in Marshallville."

"Have you thought about organizing a group here?" Mr. Fillmore suggested. "I might be able to help you get it started."

"That's a great idea!" Mayor Goodwin added with enthusiasm. "We need Special Olympics in Bluesky. We can't let Marshallville show us up. See what you can do for these people, Troy."

"The Chamber might be able to suggest some businesses that can help with a little money to get you started," Mr. Dugan said.

"Here's my card." Mr. Fillmore handed a business card to Lisa. "Call my secretary, and have her set up a meeting for early next week. In the meantime, maybe we can find out what's involved in starting a Special Olympics group. I'm sure we can get this thing off the ground."

"You're the best mom in the world!" Beth Anne said as she and Lisa got in the car. "We're going to have Special Olympics in Bluesky!"

"Let's don't get ahead of ourselves," Lisa warned. "Mr. Fillmore said he would check into it. That doesn't mean it will happen."

But Beth Anne wasn't listening. She had already pulled out her scripture card and was reading it. "All things work for good for those who love God."

CHAPTER SIX

Everyone knows there are four seasons in a year. But everyone in Arizona knows there is another season called the monsoon. Officially, the monsoon season begins in the middle of June and ends the last day of September. But no one really expects to see those dark afternoon monsoon clouds until early July. During the monsoon season, the winds that usually blow from the west are shifted so that southeasterly winds bring moisture up from the Gulf of Mexico. In an area that is dry most of the year, the monsoon rains are a welcome sight. The parched grasslands seem to be transformed into a carpet of verdant green almost overnight. And on the forest floor, ferns and flowers that have lain dormant for most of the year suddenly spring to life.

While the people of Arizona are praying for rain, they know that sometimes a monsoon storm can be just a noisy threat leaving behind the unfulfilled promise of showers. With those dry storms comes the danger of lightning that can spark a forest fire in the dry underbrush. With steep, rugged mountain ranges that stretch across large portions of the state, firefighters are forced to make their way into almost inaccessible areas. They risk their lives to contain the fire before it burns out of control destroying thousands of acres of chaparral or ponderosa pine forest.

While the monsoon season might have been on the minds of some residents of Bluesky, most of them were just enjoying the sunshine and a sky that was deep-ocean blue, streaked with waves of foamy white clouds—in other words, just another typical Bluesky day.

A large group had already gathered at the senior center by eight o'clock. Most of the seniors were dressed in blue jeans and plaid shirts with hankies in their back pockets. Many of them were sporting straw hats and even suspenders. "It's sort of our peach-picking uniform," Gus said with a laugh when he saw the Handy Helpers staring at the seniors.

"I told everyone to wear their Handy Helper shirts and jeans," Logan said. "So I guess that's *our* uniform."

"You look like a team," Walt pointed out, "and we're glad you're here to help."

The Handy Helpers were happy to see Betty and Doris, who had joined their little group, in front of the senior center. That is to say, everyone was happy except Beth Anne.

"What's the matter?" Laura asked her friend when she heard a loud groan come from Beth Anne.

"My grandma's here!" Beth Anne stomped her foot. "My mom told her to come 'cause she doesn't trust me not to climb ladders."

"Amber and Laura," Walt said, in an official tone, "*you're* going with Doris. Spike and Logan will be going with Gus. *Betty* will take Melissa and Beth Anne." Walt looked at Beth Anne as a smile spread across her face. "See," he said, "your mom does trust you."

The peach pickers piled into vehicles and headed for various parts of Bluesky. Logan and Spike were happy to squeeze in next to Gus in his Ford Ranger pickup. "We're assigned to Warren Pritchard," Gus informed them. "He has three big peach trees in his backyard."

Gus stopped his truck in front of a small house with brown siding. Paint was peeling from the dark-brown trim around the windows and door, and the roof was missing more than a few shingles. The blinds were pulled tightly shut, and a rusty No Trespassing sign hung on the chain-link fence. "Warren has some memory problems," Gus said, opening the gate, "so I'd better go talk to him first to make sure he remembers we're coming."

Logan and Spike waited next to the pickup, watching Gus as he talked to Mr. Pritchard on his front porch.

"There's something weird about his hair," Spike said, watching as Mr. Pritchard seemed to be moving his hair around on his head.

"I think it's a wig," Logan replied after studying it for a few minutes.

"Yes," Gus said with a grin as he returned to his truck, "Warren has a toupee."

"A what?" Spike asked.

"You know, a hairpiece. Not everyone is as comfortable in their own skin as I am." Gus laughed, lifting up his straw hat to rub the top of his bald head. "Warren has been wearing that rug for as long as I've known him."

"Does he know he isn't fooling anyone?" Logan asked.

"I doubt it." Gus laughed again. "And nobody's gonna tell 'im either."

Gus took a ladder and some wooden boxes out of the back of his truck. "Let's get started."

The guys had been picking peaches for about forty-five minutes when Gus received a call on his cell phone. "That was Hank," he told the boys. "Norman got stung by a bee and slid off the ladder. They're working a few blocks away. I've gotta take the first-aid kit over there and fix his bee sting and scraped leg."

With that, Gus got in his truck and drove away. Spike and Logan continued picking peaches. "These peaches smell so good," Spike said. "Do you think it would be okay if we ate one?"

"There's plenty of them." Logan was standing next to a tree with branches so loaded with peaches they touched the ground. "I'm sure no one would miss a couple of peaches."

They each pulled a peach from a tree and washed it at the faucet. The peaches were amazingly sweet and juicy. "This tastes so good," Spike said. "Maybe we can take some home when we're finished."

"That would be great," Logan agreed. "Maybe my mom will make a peach pie."

The boys were still enjoying their peaches when they heard a pounding noise coming from a window in Mr. Pritchard's house. They looked up to see Mr. Pritchard shaking his finger at them. His hair seemed to move up and down with the movement of his finger. Suddenly Mr. Pritchard's face disappeared from the window and reappeared at the back door.

Raising the broom he held in his hand, Mr. Pritchard shouted, "Don't you move! The police are on their way. I'm tired of you kids stealing my peaches!"

"But . . . but . . .," Logan stammered.

"Whatever you're trying to say, save it for the police. This time I caught you in the act. You two are in big trouble!"

Within ten minutes, a police car pulled up in front of Mr. Pritchard's house. As the officers came through the back gate, Spike and Logan let out a sigh of relief. They immediately recognized Officer Mills and Officer Fillmore. Officer Mills was a hefty man in his midforties with a red face and short brown hair. Officer Fillmore was a tall, slim black woman with a pleasant smile. Both wore uniforms. They were the police officers who had been on duty when Beth Anne was lost. "I hope they remember us," Logan whispered to Spike.

"Yeah, they'll know we wouldn't steal peaches," Spike whispered back.

"What seems to be the problem?" Officer Mills asked.

"These two boys were stealing peaches off my tree. They even had the nerve to stand here and eat some!"

Officer Mills looked at the half-eaten peaches in their hands. "What do you boys have to say for yourselves?"

"We're helping the senior center pick peaches," Logan tried to explain. "Gus brought us here."

"If you're supposed to be picking peaches," Officer Mills asked, "why are you eating them?"

"They smelled so good," Spike was finally able to speak. "We just wanted to taste one."

"You boys look familiar," Officer Fillmore said. "Aren't you friends of Beth Anne?"

"Who cares who their friends are?" Mr. Pritchard shook his broom toward the boys. "They're stealing peaches. Haul them to jail!"

"Sorry," Officer Mills looked sadly at the boys. "If Mr. Pritchard presses charges, I'll have to take you in."

"I'm pressing charges!" Mr. Pritchard insisted. "So take them away!"

"What's going on?" Gus asked as he hurried through the gate. "Did someone get hurt?"

"These boys were stealing peaches off Mr. Pritchard's tree," Officer Mills explained. "He's pressing charges. So I'll have to take them in."

"Warren," Gus said patiently, "do you remember me telling you I'd be out here picking peaches with two boys?"

"I remember you said *you'd* be picking peaches. I don't remember anything about any boys."

"We did have permission," Gus assured the officers. "These boys are volunteers at the senior center. See, it says so on their shirts."

"That's right!" Officer Fillmore smiled. "These boys are Handy Helpers. They help out at the senior center."

"I had to leave for a bit," Gus explained. "That's why they were here alone."

"Everything seems okay to me," Officer Mills turned to Mr. Pritchard. "Is everything okay with you?"

"Yeah, I guess so. I'm going back in the house. Go ahead and pick the peaches. Just don't let those boys eat them all."

"Don't worry about that," Spike said with a groan. "The way my stomach feels right now, I don't think I can eat *anything*!"

After another hour of peach-picking, Spike and Logan sat down under a tree and took out their lunches.

"That was a close call with the police," Logan said, chewing a bite of sandwich.

"As close I ever want to get to going to jail," Spike agreed. "That was really scary."

"How about going fishing tomorrow," Logan suggested. "We could get an early start and maybe catch some big ones."

"Sorry," Spike groaned, "I'm busy on Friday. What about Saturday?"

"I promised my mom I'd go with her to the farmers' market in Marshallville. What's going on Friday?"

"I'm spending the day at Todd's. He's coming to get me at nine o'clock."

"I thought you didn't like Todd," Logan sounded confused. "Why are you going to his house?"

"He invited me in front of my mom," Spike explained. "She wouldn't let me say no. She thinks spending time with a teenage role model will be good for me."

"Todd's a role model?"

"My parents think so. They don't know what he's really like."

"Why don't you tell them what he's really like?"

"I've tried, but they think I'm just blowin' smoke. Todd's like super nice when he's around my family. But when we're alone, he totally changes. He's always punching me or calling me a weirdo. Mom says that's how he messes around with his older brothers, but I hate it!"

"Todd's a bully. You shouldn't let him get away with it."

"Don't worry. I can handle him. He's on his way out anyway. Jennifer only has a boyfriend for three months. His days are numbered."

"What if Jennifer gets serious about him?"

"That won't happen. She could never get serious about a bonehead like Todd."

Beth Anne and Melissa climbed into the backseat of Betty Jenkins's mint-green Volkswagen bug. "Are you glad to have your cast off?" Betty asked Beth Anne.

"Yes, I am!" Beth Anne exclaimed. "It was so itchy."

"You got it off just in time to do all the things you like to do in the summer," Betty continued.

"I can't ride my bike yet, but I can go swimming."

"Have you been to the Bluesky pool?"

"No, but I'm going to practice for Special Olympics at the Bluesky pool."

"I thought you had to go to Marshallville for Special Olympics," Melissa said, suddenly interested in the conversation.

"No, I forgot to tell you. My mom is getting us a team here. She said that you can be on the team too."

"I don't think so," Betty said. "Special Olympics is just for kids in special ed."

"No, it's not," Beth Anne corrected her. "My mom said that Melissa can be on our team. There are four kids on the team, and Melissa can be on it."

"I'm sure your mom knows what she's talking about," Betty said, not wanting to upset Beth Anne.

"'Cept we don't have a coach," Beth Anne went on. "We have to have a coach."

"Isn't your mom going to be the coach?" Melissa asked.

"No, she said she's not a good swimmer. Mrs. Markham is helping too. But she's not a good swimmer either. Maybe you could be our coach, Betty."

"I grew up in Kansas. I didn't do a lot of swimming. I wouldn't know anything about coaching. But I know who would. I'm surprised you didn't think of it, Melissa—your grandmother Sarah. She was on her high school and college swim teams."

"That's right!" Melissa said, excited. "She even had a chance to be in the Olympics. She showed me her photo album. She's a great swimmer!"

"Can you ask her to be our coach?" Beth Anne grabbed Melissa's arm.

"I'll ask her," Melissa promised, "as soon as I get home."

"Who lives here?" Beth Anne asked as Betty stopped her car in front of a small white house with a big front porch and two huge elm trees in the yard.

"Victor and Helga Schmidt," Betty told her. "We're going to pick peaches in their backyard. They're a very nice couple. I know you'll like them."

A short man with a round face, white hair, and a white mustache answered the door. "So nice to see you," he said to Betty. "Who are your little friends?"

"This is Melissa and Beth Anne," Betty said, indicating the two girls standing on either side of her. "This is Mr. Schmidt."

Just then, they were joined by a short woman with wide hips and a wide smile. Betty repeated her introductions.

"It's nice to meet you, Mr. and Mrs. Schmidt," Melissa said.

"Yes," Beth Anne added, "I'm happy to meet you, Mr. and Mrs. Smith."

"Their name is Schmidt," Melissa whispered to Beth Anne.

"That's okay," Helga said. "Just call us *Oma* and *Opa*. That means 'grandma' and 'grandpa' in German."

"I'll get the ladders," Victor said when they were all in the backyard. "If the three of you work on that tree, Helga and I will get this one. It shouldn't take too long that way."

Melissa moved a small ladder under the tree and started picking peaches. Beth Anne stood on her tiptoes trying to reach the peaches on the lowest branches. "I can't get any peaches, Opa." Beth Anne groaned. "I need a ladder."

"I promised your mom you wouldn't get on any ladders," Betty said with a laugh. "Sorry, but you're grounded."

"Don't feel bad," Helga said. "I'm short too. Victor always hands the peaches down to me, and I put them in the box."

"That sounds like a good idea." Betty looked down at Beth Anne. "Melissa and I will hand you the peaches, and you can put them in the boxes."

Beth Anne watched as Helga collected the peaches in her apron. When she had an apron full, she unloaded them into a box. "I wish I had an apron," Beth Anne continued to groan.

"I'll get you one," Helga said, walking into the house. Within a few minutes, she was back, tying an apron around Beth Anne's waist.

"Thank you, Oma. This is much better." Beth Anne held up the apron so Betty and Melissa could drop the peaches into it.

"Don't take so many!" Betty warned. Just then the peaches rolled out of the apron and onto the ground.

"Oh!" Beth Anne said in surprise. "The peaches got away!"

"Just take a few at a time," Helga suggested. "Then they won't fall out on your way to the boxes."

The peach pickers had been working for a while when Helga announced, "I made some pork schnitzel. I hope you will all join us for lunch."

"That's very nice of you," Betty answered for everyone. "Of course we'd love to have lunch with you."

"I brought a peanut butter sandwich," Beth Anne whispered to Betty.

"You can have that any time," Betty told her. "Helga's schnitzel is a rare treat."

Melissa and Beth Anne studied the plates of food Helga set in front of them. "What is this called again?" Melissa asked, indicating the breaded meat on her plate.

"It's called schnitzel with noodles," Helga told her. "It's a German specialty."

"I like noodles," Beth Anne said happily. "And I think I like sneezle too."

"Gesundheit," Victor said with a laugh. "That's what German people say when you sneeze."

After lunch, the peach pickers went back to work. Soon the boxes that Betty brought were overflowing with peaches. Victor helped Betty load everything into her car.

"I'm so glad you came today," Helga said to Melissa and Beth Anne. "I hope you'll stop by to see us again soon. I'll make some peach strudel."

"Peach strudel sounds wonderful," Melissa said enthusiastically. "Count me in!"

"Me too!" Beth Anne said. "Good-bye, Oma and Opa. I hope I see you again soon."

"I love how your car smells all peachy," Melissa said as they drove back to the senior center.

"Would you like to take some peaches home?" Betty asked.

"Yes!" Beth Anne and Melissa shouted together.

Laura and Amber were already at the senior center when Melissa and Beth Anne arrived in Betty's car.

"We picked lots of peaches," Beth Anne announced as she and Melissa joined the other two girls.

"So did we," Laura told her. "We picked peaches at Mrs. Henry's. She asked if you had your cast off yet. She wants you to come for a visit when you can."

"Maybe I can go there tomorrow. She only lives across the street, but it was hard to visit her with my cast on."

"She's going to make us a peach pie," Amber added. "She makes the best pies. I can't wait."

Logan and Spike got out of Gus's pickup and joined the rest of the Handy Helpers. They told the girls about Warren Pritchard and how they almost went to jail.

"That sounds really scary," Amber said, concerned.

"It was until Gus got there and straightened it all out." Logan laughed. "Now it just seems funny."

Gus called them over to get some bags of peaches to take home. As they crossed the parking lot, a sudden gust of wind stirred up the dust. Gus pulled the handkerchief from his back pocket and sneezed a loud sneeze.

"Goozetight," Beth Anne said. "That's what German people say when you sneeze."

"You mean, gesundheit," Logan corrected.

"That's what I said," Beth Anne repeated, "Goozetight."

CHAPTER SEVEN

"Time to get up," Carolyn called to her son, who pulled his pillow over his head. "Don't forget, you're spending the day with Todd."

"How could I forget that?" Spike groaned as his mother walked away. Todd had promised he would make him pay. This was going to be a day of *pure torture*. "Gotta choose the right shirt for the occasion," Spike said, looking in his closet. The first shirt he pulled out said "Lazy but talented." *Not that one*, Spike thought. Then he took out a shirt that said "Don't bro me if you don't know me." Pulling the shirt over his head, he said, "Perfect!"

Spike hurried to the kitchen for something to eat. He stared into the empty cereal box for a few seconds before taking out a piece of bread and popping it into the toaster. *Maybe I should scramble a few eggs*, Spike thought. He was going to need all his strength to get through this day.

"Let's go, shrimp," Todd called from the back door. "I've got a real fun day planned." Todd was looking past Spike with a silly grin on his face. Spike turned around to see his sister Jennifer with a similar look on her face.

"Have a good time today," she said to Spike, all the while looking at Todd.

"He will," Todd assured her. "Depend on it. This'll be a day he'll never forget."

Spike grabbed the toast as it popped up and brought it with him when Todd grabbed him by the shirt sleeve and pulled him outside.

"Do you know what today is?" Todd asked as he drove down the street. "It's the longest day of the year. But for you, it might be the longest day of your life!"

Spike turned his head to look out the window. *It's gonna be the worst day of my life, that's for sure.*

Todd's friends, Chase and Andy, were sitting in the family room when Todd pushed Spike through the front door. Chase and Andy had been friends since kindergarten. Both boys were tall and slim. With dark, wavy hair and dark eyes, they looked very much alike. In fact, they were often asked if they were brothers or even twins. The only obvious difference between the two was that Chase wore glasses and Andy didn't. Andy used to wear glasses but had gotten contacts his freshman year in high school. Chase and Andy were best friends, and people who knew them were surprised when Todd started hanging out with them. Todd wasn't anything like them in appearance or otherwise. Todd was shorter and more muscular. His sandy-blond hair was always carefully styled to look like it wasn't. Todd was a flashy dresser with a walk that could only be called a swagger. When it came to personality, Chase and Andy were quiet and polite. Todd was loud and pushy. In school, Chase and Andy were almost straight A students. Todd barely got by with average grades. "Maybe they're trying to help Todd," someone suggested. "They're hanging out with Todd to look cool," someone else said. Whatever the reason, for the past two years, the three boys were often together. Now that Todd was going with Jennifer, he still managed to spend time with his friends.

"Here's our slave for the day. We can make him do anything we want."

"He's just a kid," Chase said. "Take it easy on him."

"This is payback," Todd continued. "He's gonna get what's coming to him!"

"It was just a harmless prank," Andy pointed out. "Lighten up a little."

"Harmless!" Todd gave Andy a shocked stare. "I can't even show my face at the gym!"

"Everybody's forgotten about it by now." Andy laughed a nervous laugh. "Don't make such a big deal out of it."

Todd put his hand around the back of Spike's neck and directed him into the kitchen. "I've been saving these up for a week." Todd sneered. "Just for you!"

Spike had never seen a messier kitchen. Plates and silverware caked with dried egg yolk, ketchup, and other unidentifiable food were stacked so high it was a wonder they didn't topple over. Dirty glasses were everywhere. Both sides of the sink were full of grimy pots and pans. Some of them had burned food on the bottom.

"You're not s-s-s-serious," Spike stuttered as he looked around the kitchen. "I can't clean this up. It'll take me two days."

"Well, you just have four hours, so you'd better get to work. My parents are coming home tomorrow, and this kitchen has to be spotless."

"Aren't you going to help me?" Spike groaned.

"Not a chance. This job is all yours."

Todd returned to his friends in the family room and put a zombie movie into the DVD player. "That's a pretty big mess," Chase said after a few minutes. "Don't you think we should give him a hand?"

"He'll be fine," Todd said forcefully. "He's a Handy Helper guy or something like that."

"What does that mean?" Andy asked.

"It means he's handy at doing dishes."

Todd returned to the kitchen for some sodas, only to find Spike still staring at the pile of filthy dishes. "Soap's under the sink," Todd told him. "Better use plenty to get them good and clean."

In the cabinet under the sink, Spike found a nearly full bottle of dish soap. Opening the top, he poured about a cupful into one side of the sink and turned on the water full force. Soon bubbles appeared under the pots and pans. Bits of greasy food floated to the top as the suds continued to rise. When the water level reached the rim of the sink, it spilled over onto the tile floor, carrying the slimy foam with it. The soapy white clouds spread out across the floor like a monsoon storm.

Spike pushed the running faucet to the other side of the sink and poured in another cup of soap. He watched as the suds began to pile up higher and higher. Spike picked a small skillet out of the sink. Holding the skillet by the handle, he smacked at the suds, laughing as they floated around the kitchen, eventually landing on the countertops, table, and floor. "Washing dishes is fun," Spike said out loud.

It was Andy who first came in the kitchen and saw the soapy mess. "What are you doing?" he asked in shock. "Todd's gonna explode when he sees this!"

"Let him!" Spike shot back.

Andy reached behind Spike and turned off the water. "Let's get this cleaned up before Todd sees it!"

Andy opened the door to the pantry and took out a broom. Then he opened the back door and began sweeping the soapy water out onto the patio. "Go ahead and start on the dishes, and I'll clean up the floor."

Spike had a small pile of clean pans sitting on the counter when Chase came in. "Need some help?" he asked.

"You can dry," Spike suggested.

It was about twenty minutes later when Todd realized his two friends hadn't come back. "What're you doing?" he asked, walking into the kitchen. "Michael's supposed to do that."

"We're just helping him out," Andy said. "This was too much for one guy to do alone. Grab a towel and start drying."

Todd let out a loud groan, but he did as Andy said. The piles of dirty dishes were slowly being replaced by clean ones. "Here, let me wash for a while," Chase suggested to Spike. "Your hands are getting wrinkly."

When the kitchen was all clean, Todd heated some leftover pizza in the microwave and poured sodas for everyone, including Spike. Then the boys returned to the family room and started the zombie movie again.

"What are you going to tell Jennifer about today?" Todd asked as he drove Spike home. "You're going to say something good, right?"

"You mean *lie*?" Spike looked at Todd suspiciously. "I *never* lie to my sister."

"Oh sure. I didn't think you'd have to lie. You did have a fun time, didn't you? The movie was great, and then we played foosball."

"Yeah, but what about the *dishes*? And what about you calling me your *slave*?"

"I don't see why you have to mention that. I was just joking. Can't you tell her you had a good time? If you do, I'll buy you something. How about a new baseball mitt?"

"I don't need a baseball mitt. I always tell my family *everything*. I'll make sure Jennifer knows exactly what went on at your house. When she hears about it, she'll dump you like garbage!"

"So who cares? Tell your sister whatever you want. She'll believe what I tell her, and you'll look like a dummy again!"

"Oh yeah! Well, wait and see who she believes!" Spike shouted as he got out of the car and ran into the house.

Logan chained his bike to a tree and took his fishing gear out of his bike bags. Then he headed along the winding dirt path to his favorite fishing spot on Fox Creek. The creek, flowing smoothly today, looked cool and inviting. If the fish weren't biting, he could always go for a swim. Logan passed other people fishing on the banks of the creek. He glanced into some of their buckets to see if they were having any luck. Only a few of the buckets contained fish.

Passing by the large boulders and scrubby oak brush lining the sides of the creek, Logan walked toward a sandy bank about twenty feet away. As he approached his favorite fishing spot, Logan was surprised to see someone else already there. It was a boy older than Logan. He was dressed in dirty jeans and a stained plaid shirt with its long sleeves rolled up past his elbows. The bottom of his jeans were so frayed that only a few inches of the hem were intact. On his head was a rumpled cowboy hat. His stringy hair, sticking out underneath his hat, looked sweaty and dirty. Logan tried not to stare as he noticed the boy was wearing cowboy boots that were tattered and dusty. The heels were worn almost flat, and Logan imagined there were holes in the soles.

The boy said a weak "Hi" to Logan as he continued on a short distance down the bank.

"Catch anything?" Logan asked.

"Not yet, but I caught a few yesterday."

Logan sat down on a comfortable rock and took out his fishing gear. Instead of a fishing pole, Logan noticed that the boy had a tree branch with the bark whittled off. His line was snagged and knotted. Logan was sure he had picked up a piece of fishing line someone abandoned on the bank. "What are you using for bait?" he asked the boy.

"Worms I dug up this morning," the boy answered. "Do you need some?"

"No, I brought my own bait. Thanks though." Logan baited the hook and cast his line into the water.

The boys fished in silence for a while. It was going to be a hot day, and Logan wondered where this boy lived. He didn't seem to have any drinking water with him. Was he fishing to catch food because he didn't have anything to eat?

"Hot day, isn't it?" Logan said after a long silence.

"Sure is. I was thinking about cooling off in the creek in a little while."

"Might as well," Logan responded. "The fish don't seem to be biting today."

"I guess it's too hot for them too," the boy said with a shy laugh.

"I'm Logan."

"Nice to meet you. I'm Jeremiah."

"Do you live in Bluesky?"

"No. I'm just passing through. I'll probably be moving on in a few days."

"Where are you headed?"

"I'm not sure yet. I haven't figured out where to go next. That's why I'm still here."

"Are you by yourself?"

"I don't have any parents," Jeremiah said. "They're both dead."

"Sorry to hear that. It must be tough on your own like that."

"I get by. But it's not easy."

The two boys continued to fish in silence for a while. At last, Logan laid down his pole and took out a sack lunch and two bottles of water.

"I've got two sandwiches," he said to Jeremiah. "Would you like one? They're just peanut butter and jelly."

"Sure, if you've got an extra sandwich." Jeremiah accepted the sandwich and bottle of water Logan held out to him.

"I like peanut butter and jelly," Jeremiah said with a mouthful of sandwich. "Thanks a lot."

"No problem," Logan answered.

When he had eaten half of the sandwich, Jeremiah put the other half back in the bag. "I think I'll save this for later. Sure does taste good."

After another hour without a single nibble, Logan packed up his fishing gear and headed for his bike. "No luck today," he said to one of the men who asked if he'd caught anything.

Lisa Riley pulled up in front of Melissa's house promptly at four o'clock. Beth Anne barely waited for the car to come to a complete stop before she opened the door to get out. "I'll get your sleeping bag," Lisa said, walking to the rear of the minivan.

"I can go in by myself," Beth Anne said firmly.

"Not a chance," Lisa assured her. "I have to speak to Melissa's parents first."

Melissa's little sister answered the door before Melissa could get there.

"My mom needs to talk to your mom," Beth Anne said to Melissa who came running up behind Trisha.

"I'll get her," Melissa said before turning and walking away.

"Hi, Trisha," Beth Anne said to the seven-year-old girl with blond hair and blue eyes like Melissa's. "How's Jellybean?" Jellybean was Trisha's black lop-eared rabbit.

"She's fine," Trisha said. "Wanna see her?"

Lisa waited in the entryway as Trisha ushered Beth Anne out the sliding door into the backyard.

"Do you want to hold her?" Trisha asked.

"Okay," Beth Anne said nervously. "I'll try to be brave."

Trisha showed her how to hold the feet so that Jellybean wouldn't kick.

"You're doing it just right," she assured Beth Anne.

"Where's Beth Anne?" Melissa asked when she returned with her mother.

"She went out back to see Trisha's rabbit," Lisa told her.

As the two moms chatted, Melissa went into the backyard. "Everybody's in my room," Melissa said to Beth Anne. "Come on. I'll show you what we're doing."

Melissa led Beth Anne down the hall to her room. The door was closed, but once Melissa opened it, Beth Anne saw Laura and Amber spreading clothes out on Melissa's bed. "Get lost!" Melissa said to Trisha before closing the door.

"What are you doing?" Beth Anne asked. "Are you playing dress-up?"

"We're too old for dress-up," Melissa informed her. "These clothes are for you. We're going to give you a makeover."

"A makeover?" Beth Anne repeated, unsure what that meant.

"We all brought clothes that we've outgrown," Laura explained. "You can try them on. If you like them, you can take them home."

"I like the Sponge Bob shirt." Beth Anne picked up the shirt and held it up in front of her.

"That was mine," Amber said proudly. "It looks cute with these shorts."

Once Beth Anne was dressed in Amber's outfit, Melissa showed her a flowered skirt and ruffled pink top. "You'll look classy in this one. It even has a matching hat."

As quick as she could, Beth Anne removed the first outfit and replaced it with the skirt and top. Melissa took a brush from her dresser and began brushing Beth Anne's hair. "Let's see how you look in the hat."

One after another, Beth Anne was encouraged to try on outfits until Melissa's grandmother Sarah came in the room to tell them that dinner was ready.

"Dad's grilling burgers tonight," Melissa informed them as they made their way to the backyard. Trisha came running over and took Beth Anne by the hand. "You can sit by me," she said happily.

Melissa's mother, Fran, was bringing out bowls of potato salad and chips. Sarah was busy mixing punch in a large jar. "The burgers are ready," Cody announced. "Better get 'um while they're hot."

Everyone took their seats around the picnic table, and Cody gave the blessing. "You know hamburgers are my favorite!" Amber exclaimed as she took a big bite.

"That's what I've heard." Cody laughed. "I hope I haven't lost my touch with the grill."

"Not at all," Amber tried to say, still chewing her burger, "these are great!"

Once dinner was over, Melissa wanted to return to her room to continue the makeover. "I'm tired of trying on outfits." Beth Anne moaned as she looked at the pile of clothes on Melissa's bed that was now even larger than before. "Can we do something else?"

"Don't you want to see how you look in *these*?" Melissa asked, holding up a shorts set with butterflies on it."

"I guess so." Beth Anne sighed again.

At Melissa's insistence, Beth Anne tried on three more outfits. Laura and Amber were plowing through the pile of clothes trying to decide what should be next. "How about this?" Amber held up a red-and-white skirt and top with stretchy capri pants underneath.

"No, I think she'd look great in this," Laura insisted, pointing to a green-and-purple plaid jumper with a matching purple shirt.

"Where's Beth Anne?" Melissa asked, realizing that she had quietly disappeared.

"I don't know," Amber said. "Maybe she went to the bathroom."

As Melissa walked down the hallway, she heard chatter coming from Trisha's room. Pushing the door open, she saw Beth Anne and Trisha sitting on the floor, Barbies spread out all around them. "We're playing Barbies," Trisha announced, pushing Melissa out the door and closing it.

"Beth Anne is *my* guest!" Melissa yelled through the door.

"But she wants to play with me!" Trisha yelled back.

Melissa returned to her room and told Amber and Laura that Beth Anne was playing Barbies. "I guess she's not as cool as I thought she was." Melissa sighed. "We're doing something nice for her. You'd think she'd appreciate it."

The three girls folded up the clothes and stuffed them into two large trash bags. "Do you think Beth Anne wants these clothes?" Laura asked.

"I'm sure she does," Amber said. "She was just tired of trying them on. I don't blame her. Sometimes I hate shopping for clothes. My mom drags me from store to store and makes me try on about a hundred outfits."

"I'd love to try on a hundred outfits," Melissa said gleefully. "I'd even try on two hundred, especially if I could buy them all!"

"Remind me never to go shopping with you!" Laura laughed.

Just after nine o'clock, Beth Anne returned to Melissa's room where the girls were playing music and practicing dance moves. "I have to get my pajamas on and brush my teeth."

"Why?" Melissa asked. "It's just barely nine o'clock."

"I go to bed at nine twenty-six," Beth Anne stated firmly. "I have to get ready for bed now."

"No ten-year-old goes to bed at nine twenty-six," Melissa insisted. "Anyway, you're at a sleepover. You're supposed to stay up late."

In spite of Melissa's urging, Beth Anne put on her pajamas and went to the bathroom to brush her teeth. Then she rolled out her sleeping bag and removed something.

"What's that?" Melissa asked.

"It's my night light," Beth Anne said, looking around for an outlet. "I'll plug it in over here."

"Why do you need a night light?" Amber asked.

"I always have a night light," Beth Anne said as she crawled into her sleeping bag. Within a few minutes, she was asleep.

"I guess she meant it when she said she goes to bed at nine twenty-six." Amber giggled. "Maybe we should leave so we won't wake her up."

"There doesn't seem to be much danger of that," Laura pointed out. "I think a tornado could blow through here, and Beth Anne wouldn't hear it."

CHAPTER EIGHT

Spike pulled his alb—the white robe he wore as an altar server—over the top of his dress clothes and shut the cabinet door. Then he grabbed the candle lighter, a long brass rod with a lighter and a snuffer on the end. As Spike left the sacristy to light the candles on the altar, he came face-to-face with Todd, who was picking up a church bulletin.

"Nice outfit," Todd patted Spike on the back. "Be careful you don't burn yourself."

As Spike headed down the center aisle to light the candles, he saw Todd take his seat in the pew next to Jennifer. *Todd was right,* Spike thought as he looked at them, whispering together. *Nothing I say to Jennifer is going to make any difference. Todd always wins.*

When Jennifer got home on Friday, Spike was anxious to talk to her. But Todd had picked Jennifer up from work so he had already filled her in on the day's events.

"It sounds like you had a good time at Todd's," Jennifer had said. "I heard that you watched movies and played foosball. That was really nice of you to help Todd with the dishes. He said he told you that you didn't have to but you insisted. He's such a nice guy, isn't he?"

Spike couldn't think of anything to say. Todd had covered everything that happened—at least, his version of what happened.

"How's your summer going?" Father Steve asked Spike when he returned to the sacristy. "Doing any fishing?"

"Not yet," Spike said, "I've been pretty busy."

"Well, there's plenty of summer left. I'm sure you'll get to do lots of fishing."

"I hope so." Spike let out a long sigh.

"You're not too busy to come to family night tonight, are you?" Father Steve chuckled.

"Of course not. I'll be there."

Laura was happy to see Beth Anne in church, seated between her grandmother and her mother. She was especially happy to see that Beth Anne was wearing the plaid jumper she had given her. Laura gave Beth Anne a quick wave and took a seat next to her sister Mandy.

As soon as the commentator finished the announcements, the procession came down the center aisle, led by Spike, who carried a large cross. As Spike took his place on the altar, he looked straight ahead, not wanting to make eye contact with Todd. He struggled to pay attention. It wasn't until the first reading from the book of Jeremiah that Spike perked up and listened intently. "But the Lord is with me, like a mighty champion: my persecutors will stumble, they will not triumph. In their failure they will be put to utter shame . . ." *Hear that, Todd?* Spike thought. *You can't win. You're going down in utter shame. God will get you!*

For the rest of the church service, Spike went through the motions of being an altar server. He didn't hear the second reading from Romans: "How much more did . . . the gracious gift of the one person Jesus Christ overflow for the many." He was not listening to the Gospel reading from Matthew: "Are not two sparrows sold for a small coin? Yet not one of them falls to the ground without your Father's knowledge. Even all the hairs of your head are counted. So do not be afraid; you are worth more than many sparrows." He still wasn't listening when Father Steve talked about God's great love for us and how there is no problem too small or too large that we cannot turn to God for help. Spike didn't hear any of what was said because he was too busy plotting how he was going to help God teach Todd a lesson.

Amber and her family were just coming through their front door after attending the Sunday service at the Community Christian Church when they heard the phone ringing.

"I'll get it," Kyle called out. Kyle almost always got the phone because the calls were almost always for him.

"It's for you." Kyle handed the phone to Amber. "It's a guy," he whispered.

"Hello," Amber said, with no clue who could be calling her. "Is everything all right? Is there an emergency? . . . No, I'm not doing anything. . . . I'll have to ask my parents, but it should be okay. . . . I'll let you know at the meeting tomorrow. . . Thanks for calling. . . . Bye."

So much for respecting my privacy, Amber thought when she realized her entire family had been watching her talk on the phone.

"That was Logan," she said, hanging up the phone. "His dad is taking him bird-watching on Saturday. He remembered how much I liked watching the orioles that made a nest outside my window last spring. So he invited me to go with them to look at birds. Is it okay if I go?"

"That should be fine," Mary said, looking at her husband who nodded in agreement. "It was very nice of Logan to invite you."

"It's not a date or anything." Amber looked at her brother Kyle, who was wearing a goofy grin.

"I know," Kyle said, still grinning.

Family Night at Our Lady of Perpetual Help Catholic Church was held once a month on a Sunday evening. The program began with a talk provided by Max Swann, the youth director, followed by some type of fun activity. In the summer, a large screen was usually set up outside, and a movie was shown. Families brought folding lawn chairs or blankets. Popcorn and sodas were provided by the Family Life committee. Spike and his parents, along with his sister Monica, set up chairs on one side. Laura and her family spread out some blankets near the front. They were joined by Beth Anne and her parents. Jennifer arrived with Todd somewhat later, choosing to sit in the back.

Promptly at 7:00 p.m., Max came forward and welcomed everyone to Family Night. He announced that the movie would be *Despicable Me.* A loud cheer came from the crowd. "That's one of my favorite movies," Beth Anne whispered to her parents.

"But first," Max continued, "we're going to talk about something very important." With that, he flashed some words on the screen: "A clean heart create for me, God; renew in me a steadfast spirit. Psalm 51:12."

"Why are you here tonight?" Max asked. He called on a boy in front, who said, "The movie and popcorn!" Cheers and claps came from many in the crowd.

"Our family always comes to Family Night," said another boy. "It's fun!"

"Why were you in church this morning?" Now the crowd grew quiet.

"We have to go to church every week to stay right with God," a mom suggested.

"So it is your responsibility as a Christian, right? Maybe you come because it is part of your routine or because your parents make you come. Do you ever sit in church and wish that it would get over soon?" Heads were nodding as Max continued. "Why do you think God wants us to come to church?"

"To spend time with him," a young girl suggested, "because he loves us."

"That's exactly right." Max smiled. "God wants to have a relationship with each of us. He invites us to his house so we can spend time with him. You are all good kids, and I know you try to do what's right. But have you ever thought about why you choose what is right?"

"Because I learned in church," said a boy in the crowd.

"My parents teach me what is right," another child added.

"It hurts God when we do something wrong," an older child said firmly.

"Yes, it does," Max agreed. "And it also hurts us and our relationship with God. But God loves us so much, and he calls us to love him. He wants to help us choose to do what is right. He wants us to call on him when we have problems. Our Heavenly Father knows that it is hard for us to always choose the best way to go. That is why we have to depend on him for all things and put him above all else. As the scripture says, we should ask God to create in us a clean heart. But that can only happen when we spend time in prayer and come to mass with a desire to be there—in other words, with a steadfast spirit."

Max encouraged families to discuss this topic further at home. "There's a handout for you to take home. It has questions you can discuss as a family. And now for our movie!"

Spike and Logan looked at each other with concern when they walked into the senior center for the weekly meeting of the Handy Helpers. Coming out of Walt's office, they saw Officers Mills and Fillmore. "I wonder what they're doing here," Logan thought out loud.

"I hope it doesn't have anything to do with Mr. Pritchard's peaches," Spike completed his thought.

"We'll do what we can," Officer Mills said to Walt.

"I know you will," Walt responded. "I hate to think there's a thief in Bluesky."

Logan and Spike looked at each other again. "Maybe Mr. Pritchard pressed charges after all," Logan said. "Do you think they're here to arrest us?"

"Maybe we should make a run for it," Spike suggested.

"Hi, there," Officer Fillmore smiled and waved at Spike and Logan. "How's it going?"

"Fine," they both said together, heaving a sigh of relief. "We thought maybe we were still in trouble with Mr. Pritchard," Logan said.

"No." Officer Fillmore shook her head. "We're here on another matter."

"Someone stole the food we had stored out back—a box of canned goods. It was supposed to go to the food bank," Walt explained. "I can't imagine why someone would do that."

"Did you find any evidence?" Spike asked.

"Just a lot of footprints. Some of them are Bob's, and some are mine. But a lot of people walk through there. It's sort of a shortcut. There are plenty of sneaker prints, sandals, and even cowboy boots."

"Cowboy boots?" Logan asked, surprised. "I don't see too many people wearing cowboy boots."

"Sure," Officer Mills said. "There's at least ten horses in the town stable. All the horse owners wear cowboy boots."

"Do you think one of them stole the food?" Spike asked.

"No, I'd be surprised if it was anyone living in Bluesky," Officer Mills explained. "I expect if we catch the thief, it will turn out to be a stranger."

"Maybe we can help," Spike suggested, "you know, keep our eyes open for anyone suspicious."

"Better leave that to the police," Officer Fillmore said. "The thief is probably long gone by now anyway."

"I'm glad you are all here today," Walt said as the Handy Helpers took seats around the table in the copy room. "The Fourth of July is next week, and I'm hoping you'll be able to help us out with some of the activities."

The Fourth of July was a big day in Bluesky, beginning with a parade down Main Street and ending with a fireworks spectacular. In between were lots of games, picnics, music, and fun.

"First of all," Walt began, "would you like to be in the parade with us?"

"Sure we would." Logan looked around the table at everyone. They were all nodding, except Laura. "I have to be on the float with my mom's dance studio. I know she'll never let me out of it."

"And we don't want her to," Walt said. "I'm just asking if you would like to be in the parade with us, but only if it's okay with your families."

"Sure," Logan said. "Everyone who can will be there."

"I'd like you to help with three events at the park. First, we need someone to serve pie. The ladies will be making lots of them—especially peach—and we're going to be selling them by the slice."

"I'd like to do that," Laura offered.

"So would I," Melissa added, "especially if we get to sample some."

"That's entirely likely." Walt laughed. "We just need you to cover the noontime shift so the ladies can have a break. Would that be okay?"

"Sure," Melissa said, "pie for lunch. I'll take that any day!"

"Then we need some help with the watermelon-eating contest. Troy Fillmore, the town manager, is the reigning champion. He won it in a minute and ten seconds last year."

"The guys can take that one," Logan said with assurance. "Chris is coming home on Wednesday, so he can help out."

"Sure," Spike added. "I like to see them trying to eat watermelon without using their hands. It's pretty funny."

"The watermelon will already be cut up. All we need is for you to put the slices in front of the contestants," Walt explained.

"What about us?" Beth Anne and Amber asked together. "Don't you have anything for us to do?"

"I have something really special for you." Walt smiled. "You can help with Bark in the Park."

"You mean the dog parade?" Amber asked. "I didn't know they were having that again this year."

"Yes, they are," Walt continued, "and I thought maybe you would lead the parade."

"Sure!" Amber said, excited, "I can bring Domino!"

"But I don't have a dog," Beth Anne said sadly.

"Maybe the Andersons will let you borrow Cher," Amber suggested.

Wednesday morning was the first practice of the Bluesky Special Olympics swim team. Everyone was there at nine o'clock. Mr. Fillmore had arranged the use of the pool for free, and Melissa's grandmother Sarah had agreed to be the swim coach. Mrs. Markham, the special education teacher, and Mrs. Barrows, her aide, were on hand to help the swimmers, like Joey, who required more assistance in the pool. Joey had just turned eight years old, which made him old enough for Special Olympics. Because he has cerebral palsy, he was not able to swim across the pool, but Lisa assured Joey's mom that there were events he could participate in.

Besides Joey and Beth Anne, other students from Mrs. Markham's class came to join Special Olympics. Shelly was there to practice even though she would have to wait until next year when she would be old enough to compete. Willy, a nine-year-old boy with Down syndrome like Beth Anne, was eager to show how well he could swim. Another boy named Sam liked to splash in the water but was afraid to go in all the way.

"We'll see if we can't help him get over his fears," Sarah said patiently. "In the meantime, he can do whatever he is able and willing to do."

Beth Anne was correct when she said that Melissa could participate in Special Olympics—as a member of a unified relay team. The team would be made up of two Special Olympic athletes and two partners. Beth Anne and Willy would be the athletes. Melissa and Joey's big sister, Brianna, would be the partners.

"How's your summer going so far?" Melissa asked Brianna as they waited by the pool.

"Okay, I guess. My mom's been busy with Joey, so I haven't gotten to do much. I'm glad I get to be on the swim team." Brianna had been in their class at school, and Amber and Laura thought she was nice. Melissa didn't want to be friends with Brianna at first because it seemed like she was always telling everyone what to do. Melissa said that Brianna smiled too much on purpose to show off her dimples and that her dark hair was too curly. Now that Melissa and Brianna knew each other a little better, they promised to try harder to get along. They both knew that Beth Anne would make them keep their promise, especially now that they were going to be teammates.

"Joey's signing something," Melissa pointed out as she watched Joey's fingers moving quickly.

"He's signing your name, Melissa," Brianna said. "You know he has a big crush on you."

"Yeah, I remember he wanted to be my boyfriend." Melissa laughed. "My parents won't let me have a boyfriend yet," Melissa said to Joey.

Joey pointed to his chest and then twisted his hands like he was ringing out a wet rag.

"Let me guess." Melissa smiled at Joey. "You said I broke your heart."

Joey made a fist and then shook it forward twice. "That means yes," Brianna said. "You broke his heart."

"Before we begin," Sarah announced when everyone was seated in the picnic area at the pool, "I have a few rules. First of all, when I'm talking, I need everyone to listen. Swimming is lots of fun, but being around water can be dangerous. I need you all to pay attention. When I blow this whistle, I want you to stop, look, and listen. What are you going to do when I blow the whistle?"

"Stop, look, and listen," the swimmers repeated.

"Very good. There will be no running in the pool area. The deck could be wet and slippery. We don't want anyone to fall and get hurt. The next rule is to keep your hands to yourself. We all have different abilities and fears in the water. We must respect one another. Is that clear?"

"Yes, coach," the athletes responded.

"We will be practicing for two hours every Wednesday morning. I need you to be on time because we have to be out of the pool by eleven o'clock. We will begin each session with a warm-up. For the first few weeks, I will be assessing your skills to find out how well you swim. Later, we'll decide what events you will be in, but for now, we'll just be working on the basics. Are there any questions?"

"What if I get water in my eyes?" Shelly asked.

"That is a problem when you're swimming under water," Sarah told her. "We're going to try to get some goggles for you to wear."

Sarah led the athletes in an aerobic warm-up that consisted mostly of marching in place. Then they did some stretches. Finally, everyone was told to get in the water. There was so much excitement; they were splashing water and grabbing at each other. Sarah blew her whistle loudly. Everyone stopped and looked at her.

"Very good," she said. "You remembered what to do when you heard the whistle. What was the rule you forgot?"

"Keep your hands to yourself." Beth Anne hung her head. "I'm sorry. I forgot."

"That's okay this time." Sarah smiled. "But we have to remember the rules and remember to act like a team."

Near the end of the practice, Troy Fillmore, dressed in a white shirt and tie, came into the pool area and walked over to watch the athletes as Sarah led them in their cool-down.

"How did it go today?" Troy asked Lisa.

"Just fine, I think," Lisa answered, looking at Sarah for confirmation.

"The kids were great," Sarah said. "I think we'll have a very good team."

"Are there any things you need?" Troy asked.

"Yes, as a matter of fact, there are," Sarah told him. "We need goggles and kickboards and a stop watch."

"Make me a list of what you need," Troy said. "I'm sure I can get the businesses in town to donate money to buy everything."

"Thank you so much," Lisa offered her hand to Troy, who returned her handshake. "None of this would have been possible without your help."

"It was my pleasure." Troy smiled and looked around at the athletes, wrapped up in their towels. "It looks like a winning team to me."

Logan and Spike were waiting at Chris's house when his family's Tahoe pulled up in the driveway. "How was California?" Logan asked as soon as Chris was out of the car.

"It was fantastic!" Chris said, excited. "We could walk to the beach from my grandparents' house. I even tried surfing a little. Grandpa showed me how. My grandparents took us to Disneyland and Hollywood."

"You're back just in time for the Fourth of July," Logan filled him in. "We're gonna be in the parade and help with the watermelon-eating contest."

"That'll be fun," Chris said. "What have you been doing while I was gone?

"We picked peaches at Warren Pritchard's house," Spike told him.

Spike and Logan took turns explaining how they almost got arrested for stealing peaches.

"That's a crazy story," Chris said. "Good thing it all worked out."

"We thought for a while it didn't work out," Spike continued. "When we went to the senior center on Monday, those two police officers were there. We thought we might be going to jail after all."

"But they were there because someone stole some cans of food," Logan explained.

"Really? Who would do that?"

"The police think it was somebody passing through town, a stranger wearing cowboy boots." Spike kind of laughed.

"The weird thing is, I met a stranger wearing cowboy boots," Logan told them.

"Really?" Spike was surprised to be hearing this for the first time. "Where did you meet him?"

"At Fox Creek when I was fishing. He was real dirty and wearing some old cowboy boots and a cowboy hat."

"Do you know his name?" Chris asked. "Maybe you should tell the police."

"His name's Jeremiah," Logan continued his story. "He's a teenager. He said his parents are dead and he's on his own. He said he's just passing through. I'm sure he's gone by now."

"We still should tell the police," Spike insisted. "Just in case he's still around. He might be dangerous."

"He looked really poor," Logan said, "and hungry, not dangerous at all. If he stole the food, he really needed it."

"If I see him," Spike said adamantly, "I'm calling the police!"

Todd was working on Saturday, but Jennifer had the day off. She and Monica decided they would look totally cute in tie-dyed shirts at the Fourth of July celebration. Monica remembered her world history teacher telling them about the natural dyes the Egyptians used. She did a web search and came up with some vegetables they could use to make dyes.

Spike smelled something strange when he came into the kitchen. "What are you cooking? It smells like garbage."

"It's red cabbage," Monica said. "We're using it to make blue dye."

"If it's red cabbage," Spike asked, "wouldn't it make red dye?"

"No, the red dye's in there." Jennifer pointed to another pot cooking on the stove.

"Is that blood?" Spike asked when he looked in the pot. "Did you kill an animal and drain its blood?"

"Of course not," Jennifer said. "We're cooking beets."

"I hope that's not dinner!" Spike wrinkled his nose.

"We're making red dye, I told you." Jennifer was getting impatient with her brother. "Now get out of here before you knock something over!"

Spike went to the backyard and played with Tigger for a while. When he walked back through the kitchen, he saw his sisters pouring red and blue dyes into small bottles. Later, he saw their tie-dyed shirts hanging in the backyard.

"Your shirts look pretty cool," he said at dinner. "Maybe I should make one for the Fourth of July."

"We had dye left," Monica offered. "It's in the cabinet in the laundry room. You can use it if you want."

"Speaking of the Fourth of July," Carolyn said to her family, "we should probably see what everyone has going on so we can coordinate our activities."

"Todd and I will probably hang out at the pool," Jennifer said, "and then we'll go to the fireworks."

"My softball team is having an exhibition game at six o'clock," Monica informed her family.

"We should all definitely be there for that." Carolyn made notes on the message board. "And of course, we'll all be at the fireworks."

"I'm going to be in the parade," Spike announced proudly, "and I have to help with the watermelon-eating contest in the afternoon."

"Todd'll want to be in the watermelon-eating contest," Jennifer said. He loves watermelon."

"We should all plan to go to the parade, the softball game, and fireworks. Otherwise, you're on your own for the rest of the day. If you need anything, your father and I are going to play scrabble with some friends in the park and try to stay cool."

CHAPTER NINE

Clowns, clowns, and more clowns—everywhere Logan looked, there were clowns. "Did you all join the circus?" he asked as he walked up to someone he thought might be Gus.

"These are just our costumes for the parade." Gus laughed. "How do I look?"

Gus had green-and-orange hair, a red rubber nose, and a big smiley mouth. His oversize pants were stuffed and held on by oversize suspenders.

As the other Handy Helpers arrived, they were surprised to see so many of their friends from the senior center dressed as clowns. There were clowns with giant shoes on their feet trying to ride little trikes. Amber recognized Betty Jenkins right away even though she was wearing a bushy yellow wig and her face was painted white. Her baggy green dress was covered by a rainbow-striped apron, and her pants had one pink leg and one blue leg. Hank and Clarisse Anderson were dressed as Raggedy Ann and Andy. They were both wearing wigs made out of red yarn. Hank wore a plaid shirt with a big white collar. Clarisse had on a dress that matched Hank's shirt, a white apron, and white bloomers with red-and-white-striped socks.

"Did you make your costumes?" Melissa asked.

"Yes, I did," Clarisse said. "What do you think?"

"They're so cute! You are the perfect couple! And look at you!"

Melissa bent down to take a closer look at their dark-brown toy poodle, Mon Cheri—or Cher, as the Andersons called her. She was wearing a tiny version of Clarisse's dress and socks. "How adorable. Do you remember me? I'm Melissa."

Apparently Cher had a memory lapse because she snapped at Melissa, who backed away. "Shame on you! This is one of your babysitters," Clarisse scolded. "Now give her a big kiss."

Melissa bent down, and Cher gave her a sweet lick on the neck. "I guess she does remember me after all."

"Would you like to be clowns?" Walt asked as the Handy Helpers assembled in front of the senior center.

"Can we?" Amber jumped up and down with excitement. "That sounds like so much fun!"

"We've got a whole closet full of clown costumes. You can pick out what you want."

Chris found what he called a clown tuxedo with bright plaid pants and long tails. "I'm wearing this," he said. He completed his outfit by adding a black top hat and a big red nose.

Spike chose some oversize denim shorts with patches on the back and suspenders. Then he put on a green wig and cowboy hat.

"You look like a rodeo clown," Logan told him. "Maybe you can get a job at the rodeo in the bull-riding arena."

"Not me!" Spike exclaimed. "I'm not getting stabbed in the butt by some bull's horns!"

Beth Anne wanted to look like Mrs. Henry who was dressed as a clown pirate. "That's better than looking like your grandmother." Amber laughed. Doris was dressed like a bag lady, complete with a grocery cart full of junk.

"This is just like playing dress-up." Beth Anne giggled as she plowed through a large box full of clown clothes.

"We're too old for dress-up," Melissa reminded her. "Let's just call this a clown makeover."

Before it was time for the parade to begin, the Handy Helpers emerged from the storage room looking every bit as silly as the seniors.

"We're all ready," Logan announced. "What do we do now?"

Walt gave the Handy Helpers plastic bags full of little American flags to hand out along the parade route. As the seniors and the Handy Helpers took their places in the parade lineup, Logan had a new concern.

"We're right behind the Shady Ladies," Logan whispered to Gus.

"That's right. But they're not real saloon girls," Gus pointed out. "Those are just costumes."

"But they're on horses," Logan continued to be concerned.

"So you'll just have to watch where you step," Gus said with a grin.

"Don't worry about it," said Bert, who overheard their conversation. "That's what me an' Norman are here for. We have shovels and buckets. We'll keep the road clean."

As the Handy Helpers waited for their turn in the parade, they were able to see the floats and other entries that were passing by. They waved to Laura as her mother's dance school float came into view. Some of the dancers were walking in front, wearing red, white, and blue leotards. As they marched along, some of them did cartwheels or handstands. Laura was seated on the float that was covered with red, white, and blue balloons. She and the other dancers on the float tossed candy to the children along the parade route. Amber's brother, Kyle, was on the Community Christian Church float. He was playing his guitar as choir members sang "America the Beautiful." In addition to the floats, there were walking groups carrying banners. Children who had decorated their bikes with red, white, and blue streamers were riding along with parents pushing strollers with similar decorations.

Mayor Goodwin and his wife were seated on the back of a 1955 red Chevy convertible with white interior. He had a white T-shirt stretched over his ample belly and a black leather jacket that was a few sizes too small. Mrs. Goodwin wore a poodle skirt and a sweater set with a scarf tied around her neck. "Do you think they wore those clothes when they were teenagers?" Melissa asked her friends.

"Probably," Spike said. "He must have been a smaller guy back then."

There were buggies and horse-drawn carriages, as well as little carts pulled by miniature horses. An old fire truck went by, carrying the town council members. "Get ready," Walt called out as the Shady Ladies began to move forward. Bert and Norman scurried around to clean up what the horses left behind as the seniors and the Handy Helpers walked along the edge of the crowd or rode their trikes down the middle of the street. Little children squealed with delight as the clowns came forward and handed them flags. Occasionally, someone would ask one or two of the Handy Helpers to pose for pictures. "Maybe we'll be in the newspaper," Melissa said, hopefully.

"It won't matter," Amber pointed out, "'cause nobody will know who we are."

After about a mile, the parade came to an abrupt end as the participants scrambled to get out of costumes or locate their vehicles. The Handy Helpers made their way back to the senior center to return the costumes and get their bikes. With the parade over, they were eager to get to the park for the rest of the Fourth of July celebration.

This promised to be the hottest Fourth of July on record. With no hints of monsoon rains visible in the all-too-blue sky, everyone was seeking ways to stay cool. As temperatures climbed into the nineties, seniors sought refuge under the shade trees or hoped for a small breeze off the lake. Many families were encamped at the town pool. For the young people, there was another alternative—water-gun wars. This had been a popular event in Bluesky for many years. It was started by a group of parents who brought their children to a distant corner of the park where no one would be bothered. Parents and children enjoyed hiding behind trees and bushes to attack one another with water guns. Eventually, it became an actual Fourth of July event promoted in the town brochure.

As more powerful water guns became available and older teens and young adults from outside Bluesky came to participate, the water-gun wars got out of hand. Surprise attacks were made on unsuspecting people strolling through the park, lounging under trees and even enjoying a picnic lunch. Following every Fourth of July celebration, the town council would receive a barrage of complaints about water-gun attacks. Every year, new restrictions would be imposed, but they were not specific enough, and no one enforced the restrictions, so the attacks continued and even escalated. Finally, the town council put an end to the water-gun wars. It was the year that someone with a colossal soaker gun took aim at Mr. Pritchard's toupee and blasted it clean off his head. It flew twenty feet before landing in the lap of

Mildred Parsons, who mistook it for a rodent. After jumping up and down on it for a few minutes, she kicked it in the direction of some children who were playing nearby. Before Mr. Pritchard got to it, a scruffy-looking dog picked it up in its mouth and ran off. Eventually, Mr. Pritchard was able to rescue his hairpiece from a group of boys who were using it as a hacky sack. With a multitude of similar reports, the town-council meeting was packed with irate citizens. The town council had no choice but to ban the water-gun wars entirely. Strictly enforced rules imposed punishments on anyone who brought even a tiny squirt gun into the park on the Fourth of July.

The ban was in effect for three years until a group of responsible young people and their parents petitioned the town council to let them have a small event in a controlled area. Any water guns brought to the park had to remain in the designated area. Anyone leaving the area had to check his water gun. This was the second year the event had been held, and so far, everyone was abiding by the new rules.

Spike took his super blaster drenchinator out of his bike bag and made his way to the southeast corner of the park. As he went through the entry gate, he was halted by a young man seated at a table. "Read the list of rules first. When you sign, you are agreeing to abide by all the rules." The first rule stated: *You will get wet*. Other rules warned against aiming at someone's face, continuing to hit someone who yells "Stop!" etc. "The most important rule of all," the young man pointed out to Spike, "is the rule that says you cannot take your water gun to any other parts of the park. When you leave, you must check your gun here. You will be able to get it back when you're ready to go home. Anyone caught using a water gun outside of this area will be banned for life. Do you understand?"

Spike thought the young man was just a little too intense about it all, but he agreed and signed the paper. It would have been more fun if Chris and Logan were there, but they were busy with their Boy Scout troop giving demonstrations on starting fires without matches and making biscuits in dutch ovens.

As Spike rounded a corner obscured by trees, he was hit with a blast of water. Spinning around, he aimed his blaster in the direction of the attacker. "Missed me," he heard someone call out. "Is that you, Andy?" Spike yelled as he recognized the voice of Todd's friend.

"Yeah, we're all here—me, Chase, and Todd. Better watch out. Todd's out to get you."

"Not if I get him first." Spike tried to laugh.

"That'll never happen!" Spike heard Todd shout from the other side of some bushes. "Bet you're too chicken to come 'round here!"

Spike followed the path to the other side, staying low and watching for a surprise attack from Todd. Finally he reached a clearing surrounded by large boulders. Sometimes a head would appear between two boulders, and then a soaker gun would start blasting water around the clearing.

"I'm over here!" Spike heard Todd call, but he couldn't see him.

"Where?" Spike yelled, spinning around in a circle.

When Spike stopped spinning, he was face-to-face with Todd, who had his soaker gun pointed at Spike's waist. Pulling the trigger, Todd soaked the front of Spike's shorts. "Look at Spike!" Todd called to the kids behind the rocks. "He got so scared he wet his pants!"

"I didn't wet my pants!" Spike defended himself. "You did it!"

"What a baby!" Todd taunted him. "You wet your pants. Better go home to Mommy!"

Other kids started yelling, "Spike wet his pants! Spike wet his pants!"

Faces seemed to be springing up from behind every rock, all yelling, "Spike wet his pants!"

Spike ran back around the bushes and down the path. The taunting seemed to follow him. When Spike reached the gate, he continued through. "You have to leave your gun here until you leave the park!" the young man called after him. Spike turned around and yelled back, "I *am* leaving the park!"

When Spike reached his house, he went in his room and changed his clothes. He was wishing he could hide out there until the Fourth of July was over, but he knew he would have to go back to the park. At four o'clock, he was supposed to help Logan and Chris with the watermelon-eating contest. And his parents expected him to show up at Monica's softball game at six. If he didn't, they'd want an explanation. Much as he would like to get Todd in trouble, telling his parents what happened was the last thing he wanted to do. At least, he could hang out at home for a while.

Sitting on his bed, Spike thought about how he might get even with Todd. It seemed that no matter what Spike did, Todd always came out on top. There had to be some way to turn the tables on him. It was then that a glimmer of an idea began to form in his mind. Spike remembered Jennifer saying that Todd was going to be in the watermelon-eating contest. Jennifer would be there watching in her tie-dyed shirt. He wanted to make a shirt of his own, but he didn't have time. Then he remembered bottles of leftover dye. Spike opened the cabinet, and there it was—exactly what he needed. Spike took the bottle of red dye and put it in a Ziploc bag and then into the pocket of his shorts. If this worked out, Todd would get what he deserved and then some.

Promptly at noon, Laura and Melissa arrived at the pie concession in the park. "So glad to see you girls," Agnes Henry said. "We could use a break."

"How's business?" Laura asked.

"Pretty hectic," Doris Duncan told her. "People in Bluesky sure do love pie!"

"Especially this peach pie, I bet," Melissa said, hoping she could have a piece.

"Agnes made those," Doris said. "They're our best sellers."

Doris pointed out the supplies the girls would need—disposable gloves, plates, forks, etc.

"Here's the cash box," Doris said.

"Be sure to help yourselves to a slice," Agnes told them as she and Doris were leaving.

"Thanks!" the girls exclaimed.

"We were hoping you would say that," Melissa added.

Amber had spent an hour trying to dress Domino for the parade. First, she put a straw hat on his head, but he shook it off before Amber could tie the ribbon under his chin. The blanket she put on his back was only there for seconds before he used his teeth to remove it. In the end, Amber had to settle for a flag bandana tied around his neck. Her brother Kyle brought Domino to the park just as the dogs were lining up for Bark in the Park. Amber and Beth Anne would be leading the parade. Since Beth Anne didn't have a dog, she borrowed Cher from the Andersons. Clarisse had dressed Cher for the event in a red, white, and blue tutu with a patriotic flower on top of her head. Even the leash was red-and-white-striped with blue stars.

Fifteen dogs would be participating in the parade. There was a Chihuahua dressed like the Statue of Liberty and a mix-breed dog with a patriotic collar and a big red bow tied around its bushy tail. There was a pug who looked embarrassed to be wearing a crocheted red, white, and blue cap and booties. Jennifer was there with Tigger, who was wearing a tie-dyed T-shirt just like her owner's. A schnauzer named Bosco was dressed like Uncle Sam, complete with a top hat and tails. His owner, Mrs. Brooks, was anxious for the parade to begin. She told Amber that she had to help her husband, the town butcher, set up the hotdog-eating contest. Bringing up the end of the parade was a basset hound named Wilber, whose belly almost rubbed the ground as he walked. He was wearing a banner that said, "Happy Fourth of July."

The parade began just ten minutes late, with the dogs cooperating more or less. The stroll around the park would take only about twenty minutes, even allowing for nature calls. Everything would have gone off without a hitch except for one oversight. Mr. Brooks, who was preparing for the hotdog-eating contest in the picnic area near the parade route, momentarily left a tub of hotdogs on the ground while he went to get the buns. It was Bosco who saw it first, or maybe he smelled it. Mrs. Brooks did her best to hold him back, but the desire was too strong. Tearing the leash from her hands, he made a beeline for the tub of hotdogs. Once the other dogs saw what Bosco had in his mouth, there was no stopping them. They raced to get their treat—all of them, that is, except Cher, who only ate gourmet dog food, and Wilber, who waddled over at his leisure to find the tub empty.

"I'm so sorry," Mrs. Brooks apologized over and over. "I've told Craig not to feed him hotdogs, but he does it anyway."

The dog owners grabbed the leashes and attempted to pull their dogs away. Dogs snapped and growled and chomped on the hotdogs until every scrap was gone.

"It looks like Bosco is the winner of the hotdog-eating contest!" Walt said, laughing.

Chris and Logan were already there when Spike arrived at the watermelon-eating contest. Gigantic watermelons had been cut up, and large slices were waiting for the contestants. "Last call for the watermelon-eating contest!" Mr. Howard, the president of the town council, shouted into the microphone. Contestants had already taken most of the seats at the table. Spike noticed Todd sitting on the far end and made his way there so he would be able to give Todd his slice of watermelon along with a big slice of revenge. Troy Fillmore was already in position, looking confident in his ability to win the contest for a second year.

"Before we begin," Mr. Howard said to the contestants, "I'm going to go over the rules. Your hands will remain behind your back during the entire contest. You must eat all of the red portion. Emmitt Dugan here will be the judge. He will determine when you've eaten all of the red portion. His judgment is final. We're just about ready to begin. Go ahead and set the watermelon in front of the contestants."

While Mr. Howard was speaking, Spike had carefully removed the bottle of red dye from his pocket. Using the pointed applicator, he carved a groove in a watermelon slice and filled the groove with the contents of the dye bottle. Then he set the slice of watermelon in front of Todd. Spike recognized Mayor Goodwin standing nearby. He had removed his leather jacket but was still wearing the white T-shirt.

"Okay, I think we're all ready," Mr. Howard spoke into the microphone again. "Wait a minute, there's an empty chair. Hey, Mayor, don't you want to get in on this?"

"I think I'll pass," Mayor Goodwin said, patting his belly. "I just ate a big lunch."

"Oh, come on," Mr. Howard urged. "You can't let Troy win this thing again, at least not without a challenge."

The crowd started chanting "Go, Mayor, go! Go, Mayor, go!"

At last, the mayor relented. "Okay, I guess I'll do it." The chair on the other side of Todd was vacant, but because the chairs were crowded together, the mayor asked Todd to move over so he could have the chair on the end. All the contestants had bibs tied around their necks to protect their clothing from watermelon stains. Because the mayor joined at the last minute, no one thought to give him a bib. Spike watched in horror as Mayor Goodwin took the seat in front of the sabotaged watermelon slice.

Before Spike could switch watermelon slices, Mr. Howard yelled "Go!" into the microphone. Slices of watermelon were sliding around the table as the contestants plunged their faces into the red flesh of the melons. Chomping sounds could be heard as well as groans from the spectators as they saw Troy Fillmore's watermelon slide away from him and fall under the table. Chris quickly replaced it with another slice, but Troy was now far behind the other contestants. Jennifer was jumping up and down, yelling Todd's name. Todd was focused on eating the watermelon, but his mouth wasn't as big as the mayor who was devouring every red speck in record time.

Spike, who had been watching the excitement, looked down at his hands. They were stained with the red dye. The empty dye bottle lay at his feet. Spike quickly picked it up and walked as fast as he could without drawing attention in the direction of the restroom. As he left, he could hear the crowd cheering.

"Here's the winner!" Mr. Howard shouted into the microphone, holding up Mayor Goodwin's hand. "It looks like we have a new champion this year!" he continued as the contestants were given towels to wipe their faces. "Our mayor has pulled it off for the good old red, white, and . . . red, white, and . . . bloopers! Holy moly, Mayor, what happened to your face?"

Spike quickened his pace toward the restroom. Everyone stared at the mayor, who was holding the towel in his hands.

On his face was a red smile that went from ear to ear. It wasn't a happy-clown smile but an evil, scary smile. It looked like he had been drinking blood and the blood had splattered onto his white shirt. Women nearby shrieked in terror. Toddlers in strollers and babies in their parents' arms began to cry. People came running from every direction to see what had happened.

"Better go clean up," Troy whispered to the mayor.

"You!" Mayor Goodwin called out as he entered the restroom. "It was you!"

Spike looked up from the basin where he was scrubbing his red hands and peered into the stained face of Mayor Goodwin. Their eyes locked for a moment, and then Spike broke away and ran for the door.

Mayor Goodwin examined his face in the mirror and then began washing it with soap and water. But in spite of his scrubbing, the freaky red smile remained on his face. Troy came in to check on his progress. "I think you should go home and change your shirt," Troy suggested. "You don't have any events until the softball game. You're supposed to throw out the first pitch."

At his house, Mayor Goodwin frantically went through his wife's beauty products until he found something called a facial scrub. "That should do the trick," he said. Following the directions on the container, he rubbed the paste into his skin and waited the required three minutes. After rinsing it off, he looked hopefully in the mirror, but the stubborn stain still remained. He rummaged under the kitchen sink, where he found bleach and cleanser. "Not a good idea," he said after giving them some consideration. "What about makeup? I can cover it up." Returning to his wife's vanity, he found her face powder. He dusted it generously across his face. "That looks worse!" The powder flaked from his aging skin, and the red dye quickly began to show through. At last, he opened a drawer and saw his winter-ski mask. It was a light-tan color that might just blend in with his skin. "I can cover my face with that. If I pull my cap down, maybe no one will notice."

Spike slid into a seat at the softball game, just as the announcement was made that the mayor would be throwing out the first pitch. With his head down, taking long strides, the mayor made his way to the pitcher's mound. Keeping his head down and his hat pulled low, the mayor made a wild pitch that nearly hit one of the players. Just as he was walking away, the mayor looked up into the bleachers. "He's wearing a ski mask!" someone yelled, pointing his finger at the mayor. "The mayor's wearing a ski mask!" Mayor Goodwin put his head down and left the field as quickly as he could. He was not seen again for the rest of the evening.

It was the bottom of the first inning, and Monica's team was up to bat. Spike was sitting by himself in the bleachers when he felt a tap on his shoulder. "Come with us." He looked up to see two police officers. Before he knew what happened, he was escorted to a police car. "Let's see your hands," the officer said. Spike opened his clenched fists to expose the red dye. "Guess we caught you red handed." The officer laughed sarcastically.

Spike was sitting in the police station when his parents arrived. After talking with the officer in charge, Spike was released into their custody. "You'll have to appear in juvenile court on Monday," the officer said.

Spike watched out his bedroom window as the fireworks exploded over the tops of the trees at the park. A giant red burst was followed by white twinkling stars, and then came a blue explosion. Spike couldn't keep his mind from returning to the watermelon-eating contest. *What had Mr. Howard said? Oh yeah,* "Red, white, and . . . bloopers!" *That pretty much describes my entire day!*

CHAPTER TEN

Logan felt nervous as he knocked on Amber's door. His father was waiting in the car parked at the curb. "Are you ready to go?" Logan asked when the door opened and Amber was standing there. She was dressed in denim shorts and a deep-green T-shirt that seemed to make her auburn hair sparkle in the sunlight.

"Yes," Amber said. "Do I need to bring anything?"

"Not really," Logan assured her, "we've got plenty of snacks and water and an extra pair of binoculars for you."

Logan opened the back door to the car and let Amber in. Then he walked around to the other side of the car. "Dad, this is Amber," Logan said as he got in.

"So nice to meet you," Carl said, extending his arm over the backseat and shaking hands with Amber. "I'm happy to get to know Logan's friends. I'm away from home so much I don't always know what's going on in his life."

The trio rode along in silence, Logan and Amber staring out the side windows. Carl drove to a parking lot in a wooded area to the west of Bluesky. He handed out binoculars, and they started down the sloping path that led to Fulsome Woods Riparian Preserve. "This is the best place to spot birds," Carl said. "We should see plenty."

Carl led them down a dirt path into a grove of trees. Amber looked in amazement at the massive cottonwoods stretching over one hundred feet into the air, their heart-shaped leaves quaking in the breeze. Giant willow trees draped their branches over the path. The bird-watchers stood in awe for a moment taking in the beauty. Then slowly they entered what seemed like a grand cathedral made of trees. The trio continued on, listening and watching. Carl stopped and then pointed to a nearby thicket.

Logan and Amber lifted their binoculars and tried to look in the direction Carl was pointing. Logan spotted it first. "It's a little yellow bird," he told Amber. Amber soon located the bird in her binoculars. She could hear the sweet musical sound it was making.

"That's a yellow warbler," Carl told them. "A male, I think, because of the brown streaks on its breast. The males are usually the singers."

In another thicket, Logan spotted a dark-blue bird with chestnut-colored wings. "What's that one?" he asked his dad.

"That looks like a blue grosbeak," Carl told him.

"It's so pretty," Amber said. "I love its blue color."

Logan pointed to a bird soaring overhead. "Cooper's hawk." Amber looked up to see the gray wings and white bottom.

"It looks like a young one," Carl added.

Continuing on the path, they saw a man approaching. He had a black Lab on a leash. Amber knelt down to pet the dog. "I have a black Lab too," she told the man. "His name is Domino."

"Black Labs are really good dogs," the man said.

"But your dog has better manners than Domino."

"How old is he?" the man asked.

"He's just a year old."

"Well, wait a year or two. He'll be a great dog."

The path led to a bridge that went across a creek bed that was dry this time of year. They walked into an area surrounded by smaller trees and brush. The skeletons of dead trees in among the living ones gave it kind of an eerie feeling. On the other side of the bridge, an alternate path was blocked off by a sign that read "Area closed for raptor nesting."

"What does that mean?" Amber asked.

"Raptors are birds of prey. It might be a bald-eagle nest or a falcon or even a great horned owl."

The path continued through a densely wooded area. Amber hesitated a little as the path went down steeply to a lower clearing. Logan took her hand to help her down. As the path leveled out, he continued to hold Amber's hand. Amber stared straight ahead. Her face felt warm, and she knew it was turning red.

Carl pointed toward a cottonwood tree. "You might know what that is," he said to Amber.

Amber and Logan used their binoculars to locate an orange bird with black wings. "Is it an oriole?" Amber asked.

"It is," Carl told her. "It's a Bullock's oriole."

"There was a pair of hooded orioles that built a nest in my tree," Amber said. "I hope they come back next year."

"Maybe they will." Carl nodded.

Logan pointed to a little chipmunk as it scurried through some bushes. He and Amber watched it paw at the dirt before disappearing over a log. Eventually, the path led to an algae-covered flume. The water fed a small pond that was also covered with algae and surrounded by tall reeds. There they spotted a slate-black bird with a white belly. It seemed to be wagging its tail.

"That's a black phoebe," Carl told them. "How do you like his song?"

"It's very cheerful," Amber commented.

Returning along the same path, they spotted a bird at the top of an old snag. "That's a woodpecker, isn't it?" Amber asked.

"Yes, it is," Carl told her. "It's a Northern flicker."

"He looks like he has a mustache," Amber observed.

"He sure does." Carl laughed.

Back among the trees, Amber heard a rapid, high-pitched call. "What's making that noise?" she asked.

"Let's see if we can spot it," Carl said. "It might be a chickadee or a titmouse."

"A what?" Logan asked. "You mean it's a mouse, not a bird making that sound?"

"A titmouse is a bird," Carl said, laughing. "It just has a funny name."

Finally, they saw the light-gray bird with a black-and-gray crest on its head. "There it is," Carl said. "It's a bridled titmouse."

"The flowers are pretty here," Amber observed, studying the purple, white, and orange blossoms she saw around her. Yellow butterflies were flitting from bloom to bloom. "But some of these plants look like weeds my parents make me pull up in our yard."

"They probably are." Carl laughed. "Some of these are noxious weeds, like that thistle over there." Carl pointed to a vicious-looking light-green plant with spikes and blooms like purple brushes. "Pulling weeds out of your yard actually helps control the bad weeds that can take over in an area like this."

"You sure know a lot about birds," Amber said to Carl as they drove back to Bluesky. "Thank you for letting me come along today. I had a great time."

"Thank you for joining us," Carl said. "Bird-watching has been a hobby of mine for most of my life. I always like to share what I know with others."

Spike and his parents walked through the door of the Bluesky municipal building. Spike was dressed in his church clothes. A sign on the wall directed them to the right where the court was located. Straight ahead, Spike saw a door with a sign that said Mayor's Office. He wondered if the mayor would be in court as a witness against him—wearing the incriminating evidence on his face.

His father's lawyer, Mr. Titus, met them just outside the courtroom door. "Don't worry," he said to Spike. "Everything is already worked out. The judge will probably chew you out good and then assign you community service."

Spike took a seat at the table next to Mr. Titus. His parents sat on the other side of Mr. Titus. Everyone stood as the judge entered the room. Spike was relieved that the judge was a woman, even though she was still intimidating in her black robe.

"Michael Smith," the judge began to talk, "I hope you realize what a serious situation you are in. We could be charging you with assault and sending you to the juvenile detention center. Fortunately for you, lots of people have spoken on your behalf. I understand that you are an altar server at church and that you are a volunteer at the senior center. The fact that you have never been in trouble before makes me think that you are a young man who made a terrible mistake and that you won't be making a mistake like that again. But before I pass sentence, I want to hear what you have to say for yourself."

Spike cleared his throat and started to talk. Then he cleared his throat again. All the adults in the room looked at him and patiently waited for him to say something. "I . . . I . . . I'm sorry about the mayor's face. I didn't mean for that to happen. It was just a joke, and the red dye was supposed to get on Todd. He's my sister's boyfriend. I just wanted to play a trick on him, that's all. I didn't mean to hurt anybody."

"I do believe that you weren't trying to assault the mayor," the judge said, softening her voice a little, "but you have to understand that your practical joke *did* harm someone. We can't let that kind of behavior go on in Bluesky. I want you to think about your reputation and how important it is. Once you have a reputation as a troublemaker, it is very hard to change people's minds about you. I hope you will take this seriously and protect your reputation in the future."

"I've learned my lesson, Your Honor, ma'am. I thought it would be funny, but it wasn't. I promise I will never do anything like that again."

"You do understand that you have to make amends for what you did, don't you?"

"Yes, ma'am."

"Everyone involved, including the mayor, agrees that community service is the appropriate punishment. You're going to be assigned to the Over-the-Hill gang for forty hours of community service."

"The Over-the-Hill gang?" Spike sounded worried. "Can't I just work at the senior center?"

"That will be all," the judge slammed her gavel down, and as everyone stood up, she left the courtroom.

"You can't let them do this to me!" Spike turned to Mr. Titus. "I'm gonna be chained to some big hairy guy who'll squash me like a bug!"

"What are you talking about?" Carolyn tried to calm her son. "Didn't you hear the judge? You're not going to jail. You just have to do community service."

"Yeah, chained to some killer in the Over-the-Hill gang!"

"There's the Over-the-Hill gang," David said with a grin as he pointed to Gus, Bert, and Norman, who waved at Spike. "They work on the hiking trails up in the hills. That's why they call themselves the Over-the-Hill gang."

Spike let out a long sigh of relief. "Ready to get started?" Gus asked. "We've got lots of work to do."

Bert and Norman said good-bye as they headed for Norman's car. "See you there!" Bert called out.

"Where are we going?" Spike asked once he was seated next to Gus in his pickup truck.

"We're working on the Rancho Vista Trail. It's a really nice trail with lots of pine trees. We're clearing away rocks and brush. When we're finished, the trail's going to meet up with the Sidewinder Trail."

Spike looked out the window as Gus drove up a winding road flanked on both sides by tall ponderosa pines. At last, Gus pulled off into a dirt parking area. "The trail starts here," he said. "We have to hike in two miles to get to the worksite. You can carry the shovel."

Gus took a small ice chest out of the back of his truck and started up the trail. Toting the shovel, Spike followed close behind. At first, the trail was a gradual incline. Spike looked around to see building-size boulders in among the scrub oak and manzanita. As they climbed higher, the vegetation changed to tall trees—juniper and ponderosa pines.

"How much farther do we have to go?" Spike asked as the trail became a series of switchbacks. The shovel he was carrying seemed to be weighing more and more with each turn of the trail. He carried it for a while and then let it drag behind him.

"We've only gone about a mile." Gus told him. "Hurry up. We've got a lot of work to do."

Spike had never thought of Gus as a bossy guy. He was usually just clowning around, telling jokes. But now he was hiking like their lives depended on it.

"Can't we stop for a minute and rest?" Spike asked after the third switchback.

"We need to get there and get to work," Gus said firmly. "It'll be too hot soon, and everybody will be ready to quit. I usually get here at seven o'clock in the morning. We're getting a late start because I had to wait until court was over."

"That was my fault," Spike said. "I'm sorry you got a late start."

"Well, tomorrow I'm coming to get you at six. You'd better be ready."

Spike and Gus arrived at the worksite just as the workers were taking a break. He already knew Bert and Norman. Gus introduced Spike to Frank Jones and Terrance Balfore. "Frank and Terry work for the forest service," Gus explained. "They're in charge of this operation. The Over-the-Hill gang is just here to help. We do whatever they tell us to do."

"Today we're working on removing some of these rocks and branches that are in the way. Then we'll be able to clear the path for the trail," Frank told Spike. "You and Gus can work over there." He pointed to a pile of rocks and brush a few feet from the end of the trail.

Frank and Terry worked with chain saws, cutting up a dead tree and removing it from the trail. Bert and Norman were using pruning shears to cut back some of the brush. Gus went to work, using the shovel to move the larger rocks. "Pick up the small rocks, and place them off the trail," he said to Spike.

The workers had been at it for a few hours when Frank suggested they break for lunch. Gus opened his ice chest and took

 out a sandwich and bottle of water. He handed those to Spike and then took out some for himself. The older guys sat together on nearby rocks and ate their lunch. Frank and Terry discussed their plans while they snacked on trail mix and fruit.

Spike carried his lunch to the edge of a small gully and took a seat among some rocks under a large alligator juniper tree. Below him, he could see a dry creek bed. Looking down the gully a ways, he spotted some deer grazing in the sparse green grass near the dry creek. There was a buck and

two doe. Spike opened his bottle of water and took a long, cool drink. Then he ate some of his sandwich and enjoyed the peace of the forest. Looking past the deer, Spike spotted a boy about his age. The boy looked dirty and was dressed in frayed cutoff jeans and a shirt that was too big for him. Spike stood up to get a better look at the boy who was intently watching the deer. Suddenly, the boy looked in Spike's direction. At first, they just stared at each other, but all at once, the boy began to squeeze his eyes shut, and his features became contorted as he seemed to be contracting every muscle in his face. Spike noticed the boy was clasping and unclasping his hands. Suddenly the boy threw his head back, opened his mouth, and let out a bloodcurdling scream that echoed down through the gully, frightening birds that had been pleasantly singing nearby. Spike looked back at the deer just in time to see their rumps disappear over the ridge. When Spike turned his head to see if the boy was still there, he saw that he too had disappeared.

"Did you hear that loud bird?" Gus asked when Spike returned to the worksite.

"I heard something," Spike said. "You think it was a bird?"

"Sounded like a bird to me," Bert added. "What else could it be?"

Spike wanted to tell them about the boy, but it was all such a blur. Maybe he had imagined him. Maybe it *was* just a bird.

"You're really mad at me, aren't you?" Spike asked Gus as they drove home after working on the trails.

"I'm not angry with you," Gus told him. "Maybe a little disappointed, but not angry. You made a mistake, a pretty bad one, but you have a chance to make it right and learn from your mistake."

"Are you going to give me a big lecture like my mom and dad?"

"I'm not going to lecture you," Gus said, "But if you want, we can have a talk about it tomorrow."

As Spike got out of Gus's truck, he saw Todd coming down the driveway to get in his Bronco. "Hey, there, jailbird!" Todd called out. "Are you planning any more attacks on public officials?"

Spike looked back at Gus, who smiled. "See you at six."

"I'll be ready," Spike promised.

Beth Anne arrived at the Handy Helper meeting with invitations for everyone to her birthday party on Sunday, July 14 at two o'clock at the Bluesky Bowling Center.

"You're having a bowling party!" Amber exclaimed. "That sounds like lots of fun."

"It will be fun," Beth Anne agreed. "But that's not all."

"What else is there?" Chris asked.

"Bowling is the next Special Olympics sport," Beth Anne said matter-of-factly. "I want to see who the good bowlers are for my bowling team."

"Nothing like putting pressure on your birthday guests." Melissa sighed.

"I have an invitation for Spike," Beth Anne looked around the room, "but he's not here."

"I'll take his invitation to him," Logan offered. "I was going to check in with him and see how he's doing."

"Do you think Spike can still be a Handy Helper after what happened?" Chris asked.

"I hope so," Logan said, "but I guess it's up to Walt and Mrs. Snow."

"I'll be taking it to the board of directors," Walt told the Handy Helpers. "To be honest with you, I'm not sure what they'll decide. We'll just have to wait and see."

"And hope for the best," Laura added.

"Otherwise, I think the Fourth of July celebration went well," Walt said. "Thanks for all of your hard work."

"We had a great time," Logan commented, looking at everyone nodding in agreement. "Thanks for letting us be in the parade."

"There's not much happening here this week," Walt continued. "I'm hoping you can take a break and enjoy your summer. I've got season passes to the town pool for all of you."

"Thanks!" the Handy Helpers shouted together.

"I think we'd all like to spend some time at the pool," Melissa added. "This summer's turning out to be a scorcher."

CHAPTER ELEVEN

Spike had set his alarm for 5:00 a.m., not wanting to disappoint Gus again. By six, he was waiting at the curb. When Gus pulled up, Spike jumped in his truck.

"Well, now, that's better. We'll get an early start, and you'll be able to work off more of your community-service time." Gus actually smiled a little and chatted with Spike on the way.

"If we hurry, I'll show you something I found the other day. It's pretty impressive. I think you'll be surprised."

"What is it?" Spike asked excitedly. "Is it gold? It's a great big chunk of gold, isn't it?"

"I didn't find any gold," Gus said. "But I did find something interesting."

"What *is* it?" Spike asked as he stared at the huge pile of sticks and debris. "Who piled up all this mess?"

"It's a pack-rat nest," Gus said with a laugh. "I call it a pack-rat mansion. I've never see one this big before."

"It looks more like a broken-down shack than a mansion," Spike pointed out.

"Yeah, but if you could look inside, you'd see lots of rooms like in a house. There might be a living room, bedroom and even a kitchen."

"How many rats live in there?" Spike asked. "A hundred?"

"Probably just one." Gus laughed again. "Pack rats are loners. They like to collect things, and they don't like to share."

"You mean one stingy rat built all this?"

"That's right. Kind of reminds you of people who want to have it all, doesn't it?"

"Kind of reminds me of people on the television show *Hoarders!*"

"Kind of does at that." Gus laughed.

Frank and Terry were already at the worksite, studying their plans when Gus and Spike arrived. "What're we doing today?" Gus asked.

"We're going to walk the trail or, at least, what will be the trail and see what difficulties we face," Frank said. "You can come along with us and let us know what you think. Since this trail will be used by families and older people, your opinions will be very helpful."

Spike and Gus joined Frank and Terry walking single file along the edge of a somewhat steep ravine. Terry led the way, picking the flattest route with the fewest obstacles. "This part shouldn't be too difficult to clear. I think we can finish it this week if the rain holds out."

As they continued on, they came to a burn area. It had been the location of a forest fire the summer before. A careless camper had left a fire smoldering when he packed up his camp. The fire burned five hundred acres before it was contained. "Why didn't all the ponderosa pines burn?" Spike asked as he surveyed the damaged area.

"Ponderosa pines are a marvel of nature," Frank explained. "Their bark is really thick and protects them from fire. Not only that, they automatically shed their lower branches. See how tall the trunk is before you get to the branches? It's probably twenty or thirty feet or more on some trees. If the fire doesn't burn too high, it can't get to the branches."

"I like to call the ponderosa the dessert tree," Terry said, laughing.

"Why do you call it that?" Spike asked.

"Scratch the bark like this." Terry used his fingernail to scratch a nearby tree trunk. "Now, what does it smell like?"

"It smells like ice cream!" Spike exclaimed. "It smells like vanilla ice cream!"

"I think it smells like butterscotch," Frank said.

"To me, it smells like apple pie à la mode." Terry smacked his lips.

After their hike, the group returned to the worksite. Bert and Norman were busy cutting limbs and piling them up off the trail. "Are you guys through playing around and ready to get to work?" Norman asked, grinning.

The workers spent the next two hours removing rock and debris from the trail. At last, they stopped for lunch. Gus suggested to Spike that they climb up to the top of the ridge where they would have a nice view while they ate their lunch. Gus led the way to a game trail they could follow to the top. It was a steep climb, and Spike was a little out of breath when he joined Gus in the clearing. "What's the matter?" Gus asked. "That should be easy for a young fella like you." From their vantage point, they looked down at the highway they had taken into the forest. It wound through the woods and disappeared frequently into the trees.

"We're looking at the tops of trees!" Spike exclaimed. "We must be up pretty high!"

"We are," Gus assured him. "Look over there. You can see Pine Lake. Isn't it beautiful?"

Spike looked to the east as Gus indicated. There he saw the small lake. He could even see the cement dam that held back the water. "This is so cool, Gus!"

The two found seats on a craggy granite ledge and took out their lunches. For a time, they ate in peace, enjoying the scenery and the fresh, crisp smell of pine needles. "You can start your lecture any time," Spike said. "I deserve it."

"I told you I wasn't going to give you a lecture"—Gus smiled—"and I'm not. But I would like to share something with you." Gus took a small Bible from his back pocket and opened it. Then he handed it to Spike. "Read Romans twelve twenty-one. Read it out loud."

Spike took the book from Gus's outstretched hand and located the passage. "Do not be overcome by evil, but overcome evil with good."

"Do you have any thoughts on the meaning of that scripture?" Gus asked.

"Forgive instead of trying to get even. Is that what it means?"

"That's pretty close," Gus said.

"So you want me to forgive Todd and forget about revenge?"

"You'll have to decide for yourself when you're ready to forgive Todd. But I'm going to ask you to do something—something I think will make a big difference."

"That's the kind of thing my parents say just before they tell me to do something I don't want to do."

"I want you to promise to pray for Todd every day for a week. I'm not talking about a sissy prayer like 'God bless Todd.' I'm talking about a big-man prayer. I want you to ask God to bless Todd, to grant him good health and happiness. Ask God to look with favor on Todd and take care of all his needs."

"Can I ask God to give Todd what he deserves?"

"Only if you're asking God to give *you* what *you* deserve as well."

"Okay," Spike said after thinking about it for a while. "I'll try what you said, but I don't think it will make any difference. I don't think Todd will ever change."

"Let's just wait and see what happens," was all Gus said.

As planned, the Handy Helpers met at the swimming pool on Tuesday afternoon. Monsoon clouds had been threatening every evening, and they were already building up on the southeastern horizon. "If we see any lightning," the pool attendant warned, "we have to clear the pool, and you don't get your money back."

"That's okay," Logan said. "We have summer passes."

"What's that?" Logan asked Chris as he came out of the men's shower room and headed for the pool.

"What's what?"

"What's that on your arm?" Logan pointed to a cobra snake on the upper part of Chris's right arm.

"Oh, you mean my tattoo?"

"Yeah, when did you get a tattoo?"

"When I was in California," Chris said, grinning.

"Your grandparents let you get a tattoo?"

"Yeah, it was Grandma Mo's idea. In fact, she got one too. Hers is a couple of dark-pink roses—really sweet. Grandpa was pretty steamed when he saw it."

"Your grandma got a tattoo? What did your mom say when she saw *your* tattoo?"

"She hasn't seen it yet," Chris admitted. "I don't know what she'll say if she does."

Logan and Chris joined the girls in the pool area. They all had to look at Chris's tattoo. "I can't believe you have a tattoo!" Melissa exclaimed. "Maybe I'll get a dolphin tattoo on my ankle."

"Yeah," Laura added sarcastically, "I'm sure your dad'll be okay with that!"

Chris had brought some rings that he threw in the pool so they could dive to the bottom to retrieve them. Melissa and Beth Anne showed everyone the backstroke they had been practicing at Special Olympics. The Bluesky pool had a super slide. Beth Anne was afraid to go down the slide at first, but after watching her friends, she decided to try.

"I'll catch you at the end," Laura promised. "You'll be fine."

Beth Anne was in line for the slide between Melissa and Amber. When it was her turn, she hesitated at the top so long the attendant was about ready to make her climb back down the stairs. "You can do it!" Amber urged. "Just be brave."

With that, Beth Anne sat down in the water and pushed off. When she reached the pool, Laura and Melissa were there to catch her before she went under water. "See?" Laura said. "We knew you could do it!"

By the time her mother came to pick her up, Beth Anne was going down the slide on her own. "Thanks for helping me be brave," she said to her friends.

Spike noticed huge inflated inner tubes in the back of Todd's Bronco as he waited at the curb for Gus to pick him up. "Todd and Jennifer must be going tubing on the Verde River," he said to himself. "I wish I could go tubing."

"How's the community service going?" Todd asked as he and Jennifer walked out to the Bronco.

"Okay, I guess."

"Too bad you have to work instead of having fun this summer."

"Who says I'm not having fun?"

"Yeah, right." Todd laughed as they got in the Bronco and drove away.

"Good morning," Gus said to Spike. "Ready for another day in the woods?"

"I guess," Spike sighed. "Todd and Jennifer are going tubing on the river."

"So I noticed. Would you like to be going with them?"

"Naw. I like working with you. They'd never ask me to go with them anyway."

Gus and Spike rode along in silence until Spike suddenly said, "Praying for Todd is a lot harder than I thought it would be. I guess I don't know him that well—what his plans are or anything."

"Why don't you ask him?" Gus suggested.

"He'd just tell me to mind my own business or say I was being weird."

Spike had almost forgotten about the strange boy he thought he saw in the woods until he thought he spotted him again. Frank had sent Spike down to the dry creek bed to see if there was an easy way out of the ravine. Once at the bottom of the ravine, Spike walked along the sandy creek bed to a point where it was covered with large boulders. He tried to find a path around the rocks, but the ravine was too steep and narrow. He was just about to give up and return to the worksite when he spotted something bright yellow farther down the creek. Curious to see what it was, he continued to pick his way through the rocks and debris. As he got closer, he realized it was a person wearing a yellow shirt. Thinking it might be the young boy he had seen before, he quietly crept closer. Twenty feet or so ahead of him, he realized it was a girl, maybe seven or eight years old. She had her back to him, and she was singing. Her sweet young voice rang out in the stillness—"You are my sunshine, my only sunshine." Spike watched her as she selected little polished rocks from the creek bed and arranged them on the bigger boulders.

"Find any gold?" he asked.

The girl jumped up and started to run but tripped over the large rocks in her way. "Careful," Spike said in a calm voice. "I'm not going to hurt you." Spike helped her to her feet and examined the scrape on her leg. "It doesn't look too bad. Where are your parents?"

The girl hadn't said a word, but now she started to cry. "It's okay," Spike tried to comfort her. "Please don't cry."

Spike heard footsteps coming toward them and looked up to see two boys, one taller and one that he had seen before. The taller boy stopped near Spike, who was still kneeling down by the little girl. Spike looked at the worn, tattered boots and then looked up into the face of the boy he knew was Jeremiah.

"Are you okay, Rachel?" Jeremiah asked as he picked up the little girl.

"I'm okay, Jeremiah. I fell down. This boy helped me."

Spike looked past Rachel and Jeremiah at the other boy who was standing near a big rock. He was blinking his eyes and twisting his mouth. Spike was afraid the boy was going to let out another loud scream when he suddenly relaxed his arms and stood still.

"It's all right, Daniel," Jeremiah said to him as he seemed to start twitching again.

Daniel was clasping and unclasping his hands and shaking his head. He didn't scream or say anything but made little squeaky noises like a mouse.

"What are you doing here?" Jeremiah turned his attention to Spike.

"I'm helping the guys who are working on the trail." Spike pointed up the ravine in the general direction of the worksite. "What are you doing here?"

"Me an' my brothers live here," Rachel said before Jeremiah could stop her.

"You live in the woods? Where are your parents?" Spike asked.

"Our parents are dead," Jeremiah told him. "So I have to take care of my brother and sister."

"Do you need help?" Spike questioned further. "You can go back into town with us and get some help."

"We're not going into town," Jeremiah said firmly, "and I've got to ask you not to tell anyone you saw us here."

"Why not?"

"They'll take us away," Rachel began to sob. "Please don't let them take us away."

"What's she talking about?" Spike asked.

"We shouldn't stay out here in the open. Come with me to our camp, and I'll explain everything." Jeremiah led the way to a flat area surrounded almost entirely by pine, oak, and juniper trees.

"This is our camp," he pointed to a makeshift lean-to made out of pine branches.

"You live here?" Spike asked.

"We do now, but I guess we'll be moving on sooner than we planned."

"You mean because I know where you are?"

"I made a promise to keep us all together," Jeremiah said, "and I'm keeping that promise no matter what!"

Jeremiah sat down on a large rock. Rachel sat on a smaller rock at his feet. Daniel continued to stand, still shaking his head. Finally, Spike chose a nearby rock and sat down.

"What happened to your parents?" Spike asked after a few minutes.

"Our mom passed away three years ago. She had cancer. Before she died, she made my dad promise that he would take care of us and keep us together as a family. After my mom died, Dad got a job in the copper mine in Harrison, a small town south of here. We had a little house, and everything was fine until school started. You see, my brother, Daniel, has something called Tourette's. You may have noticed how he blinks and twitches. Sometimes he makes noises. The teachers didn't like it because they said he was disruptive, and the kids called him names. Every day he was coming home crying. So when Dad got the chance at a job on the Morgan Ranch, he took it. We moved there, and everything was fine. We were too far away from any schools, so we had to get our education from an Internet school. Mr. Morgan gave us a small cabin to live in."

"That doesn't sound so bad," Spike said. "Why did you run away?"

"Our dad was out riding the fence line, and his horse was spooked by a rattlesnake or something. He got thrown from the horse and hit his head. By the time they found him, it was too late. With my dad gone, Mr. Morgan knew he couldn't legally let us stay there, so he called the authorities. Someone from Child Protective Services was coming to get us the next day. I couldn't take a chance that they'd split us up. I was afraid of what would happen to Daniel and Rachel, so we snuck out during the night. We've been traveling ever since, staying awhile here and there. I'll be eighteen in six months. Then I'm going to get a job. If we can hold out until then, I think everything will be okay."

"Are you the one who stole the food at the senior center?" Spike hated to ask.

"Yes, I did." Jeremiah hung his head. "If it was just me, I wouldn't have done it. But I couldn't stand hearing Rachel and Daniel crying at night because they were hungry. My mother was a good Christian woman. She wouldn't want me stealing, but I didn't know what else to do. The food was just sitting there, so I took it."

"That food was supposed to go to the food bank," Spike said.

"I'm sorry about that. Look, I know you've gotta do what you've gotta do, but we're gonna pack up and get out of here. I'm just hoping you can give us time to get away."

"I'm not going to tell anyone," Spike assured him. "You can stay as long as you want. I'll be working near here for a few weeks. Maybe I can bring you some food."

"I don't want you to do anything you shouldn't, but if you can forget you saw us, you'd be helping us out a lot."

"Don't worry about me telling anyone," Spike said as he was leaving. "I'll try to bring some food tomorrow."

Spike scurried up the creek bed as fast as he could. He didn't know how long he had been gone, but he knew he needed to get back as soon as he could so no one would get suspicious. The guys were all working at moving a huge rock that didn't seem to want to budge. They barely looked up when Spike came climbing out of the ravine.

"Did you find an easy way out?" Frank asked him when they stopped for a break.

"No," Spike said. "It's impossible. There's just a bunch of rocks and boulders and dead trees that washed in. It would take a dynamite blast to clear a trail through there."

"I guess we'll have to go farther down then." Frank jotted some notes in his notebook.

"Yeah," Spike agreed. "You should go a lot farther down, away from that ravine. It's no good at all!"

The afternoon monsoon clouds were moving in, and thunder could be heard off in the distance as the workers hiked the trail back to their vehicles.

"Think it's gonna rain?" Frank asked Gus.

"Not tonight," Gus said. "Probably tomorrow."

"Why do you leave all the dead trees in the forest?" Spike asked, looking around at lifeless trees that were still standing and many more that had fallen over. "It would be too hard to carry them out, right?"

"That's not the real reason," Terry explained. "There's more life in those dead trees than in the living ones. You can't see them, but carpenter ants are working away on those logs. Beetles and other insects will find homes and food there. Animals like rabbits and squirrels will burrow under the logs and make beds for themselves. Eventually, those dead trees will decompose and provide fertilizer for the forest. The standing dead—what we call snags—are home to lots of insects and birds."

"Wow! Spike exclaimed. "And I thought they were just useless dead trees!"

Beth Anne was concerned as she watched the clouds build up to the south. "What if we can't have practice today?" she asked her mom.

"Then we'll have to wait until next week," Lisa said. "There's nothing we can do about rain.

To Beth Anne's relief, the clouds remained in the distance until after the swim practice.

"I'm still assessing your skills," Sarah told the swimmers. "But next week we'll begin to determine what events you'll be in."

Mrs. Markham and Mrs. Barrows worked with the less-skilled swimmers on breathing activities, such as blowing bubbles in the water. Sarah took the four members of the relay team to a deeper part of the pool so she could assess their swim strokes. "We'll be swimming freestyle," she informed the swimmers. "I'm going to have you swim across the pool so I can see how you do."

Melissa went first, swimming quickly and smoothly, her arms and legs working together to propel her easily. Brianna was next, swimming well, although not as quickly as Melissa. When it was Beth Anne's turn, she did a sort of dog paddle, making it about half way across the pool. Sarah soon learned that Willy only knew how to float on his back.

"I guess we have our work cut out for us," Sarah said, "but if you're willing to work hard and do some practicing outside our weekly class, I think we should be ready by September."

Beth Anne and Melissa made plans to go to the pool every day. "I'm glad we got these season passes," Beth Anne said.

Brianna asked her mom to buy her a season pass so she could practice too.

"What about Willy?" Melissa asked. "We don't have a team without him, and he can't even swim."

"I know his mom," Brianna said. "I can talk to her. Maybe she'll bring him so he can practice with us."

Todd's Bronco pulled up in front of Spike's house just ahead of Gus's truck. Gus and Spike watched intently as Jennifer got out of the Bronco and walked as fast as she could toward the front door. Todd ran after her and grabbed her arm just as she was about to go in the house.

"Looks like trouble in paradise," Gus said to Spike as they watched what seemed like begging and pleading coming from Todd.

"I wonder what he did!" Spike said, amazed at the scene.

"It looks like your prediction was correct. Todd's days are numbered. That should make you happy."

"Not as happy as I thought I'd be," Spike admitted.

CHAPTER TWELVE

Jeremiah opened the last can of corn and poured it into three bowls. He was hoping to catch a rabbit in his snare, but no luck. The rain had made fishing useless. And that lady with the chickens was getting wise. He heard her say that her hens didn't seem to be laying as many eggs as usual. At least, they had corn today. But what about tomorrow? He was going to have to find food somewhere.

Above them at the top of the ravine, Jeremiah could hear the sound of the chain saw where the work crew was busy clearing the trail. He had warned Rachel and Daniel to stay in the shelter of the tree grove. He couldn't have them wandering around while he was gone. Through the trees, he saw someone walking in the direction of their shelter. Rachel had already spotted Spike and was running toward him.

"Rachel!" Jeremiah yelled. "Get back here! What did I tell you about staying in the shelter?"

"I saw Michael!" she shouted. "He's our friend!"

Jeremiah greeted Spike, who took a jar of peanut butter out of a small backpack and handed it to him. "I wish I had some bread," Spike said, "but it was hard to sneak out a big loaf. I did manage to get some crackers and a few apples."

"Thanks," Jeremiah took the food from Spike. "But you shouldn't be stealing food from your family."

"We have lots of food at my house," Spike assured him. "Nobody'll miss it. When I get a chance, I'll buy some food with my allowance."

"You don't have to do that," Jeremiah insisted. "We can manage. We're used to not having much."

"I have to get back so they don't ask too many questions about where I've been. I'll try to bring more food tomorrow."

"Mike . . . Mike . . . Michael." Spike looked past Jeremiah to where Daniel was standing. Daniel was shaking his head. "Thank . . . thank you," Daniel said.

"You're welcome." Spike smiled. "I'm glad I could help."

Logan and Chris were already at the pool when the swim team arrived. Melissa explained their plan to practice every day. Logan and Chris took Willy to a part of the pool where the water was three feet deep.

"We're going to help you practice kicking," Logan explained to Willy. "Chris will hold your hands and pull you through the water. I want you to move your legs up and down like a fish. Watch and I'll show you."

Logan dog-paddled around Willy, showing him how to kick. For the next half hour, Chris and Logan took turns pulling Willy through the water. "You're doing really good," Chris assured him. "Want to try it without holding on to me?"

Willy didn't answer but, instead, grabbed hold of Chris's wrist. "I guess we're not ready for that." Chris laughed. When the boys were tired, they got out of the pool and sat in some chairs. Soon the girls came over and joined them.

"How's Willy doing?" Melissa asked.

"We had him practice kicking," Logan said. "He's starting to get the hang of it."

"I'm learning how to move my arms and turn my head so I can breathe," Beth Anne said proudly. "Now I can swim like in the Olympics."

"She's a fast learner," Brianna added.

"I bet me and Brianna can beat you guys in a race," Melissa teased.

"Oh, yeah?" Chris grinned. "What's the bet?"

"Losers have to buy the winners a Popsicle," Brianna suggested.

"You're on!" Chris and Logan shouted together.

Beth Anne and Willy sat on the edge of the pool and dangled their feet in the water. Logan and Brianna got in the water on one side of the pool. Melissa and Chris walked around to the other side. When everyone was in position, Beth Anne yelled,

"Ready . . . set . . . go!" Logan and Brianna pushed off and swam as hard as they could.

Brianna stayed even with Logan to the middle of the pool, but then he began to pull away. He reached Chris about two arms' length ahead of Brianna. By the time Brianna tapped Melissa's hand, Chris was well ahead. Willy and Beth Anne were standing on the side of the pool cheering for the swimmers. "Come on, Melissa!" Beth Anne shouted. "You can do it!"

Melissa put her hand on the edge of the pool just seconds after Chris.

"Guys win!" Willy screamed. "Chris and Logan are the winners!"

"It's my fault we lost," Brianna said as she and Melissa walked to the snack bar to buy Popsicles for everyone.

"The guys are stronger swimmers," Melissa admitted. "If we keep practicing though, we'll take them next time."

Early Thursday afternoon, the threatened monsoon rains finally came. Spike watched the rain as it pounded against his bedroom window. Work on the trail had come to an abrupt halt as the dark clouds moved in. The workers had to make a run for it and just reached the vehicles as the rain began to come down hard. Gus's windshield wipers had seemed inadequate against the sheets of rain that were bombarding his windshield. Now sitting in his room, Spike worried about the three kids who were alone in the woods. Their makeshift home would be no protection against this rain. "They'd be better off joining the pack rat in *his* house," Spike said to himself.

About four o'clock, the rain broke for a while. Spike was watching a movie in the family room when he heard a knock on his front door. It was Logan who held out a small envelope.

"It's an invitation to Beth Anne's birthday party on Sunday. She's having a bowling party."

"I'm surprised she'd invite me after what happened with her Barbie doll.

"She's probably forgotten all about that. Anyway, she doesn't seem like the type who'd hold a grudge."

Spike invited Logan in and led the way to the family room. "I'm watching *Indiana Jones*," Spike said. "Wanna watch it with me?"

"Sure, my mom has a late nail client today, so she won't be home until six."

Spike poured them some sodas and filled a big bowl with corn chips. "I've watched this movie a million times," he said, "but I still like it."

"Me too."

It was starting to drizzle again as the movie came to an end. Logan said he needed to get home before it started raining hard. "I wish I didn't have to tell you this, but . . ."

"Let me guess. You guys are dropping me from the Handy Helpers."

"That's not exactly it, but close. Walt called me last night. They're not gonna let you be a volunteer at the senior center anymore. I'm real sorry. You can still be a Handy Helper if we have outside jobs. You just can't come to the meetings or do any work at the senior center."

"I'm not surprised." Spike let out a long sigh. "I messed up pretty bad."

"Walt said maybe after a while, the board will change their minds."

"Doubt that, but thanks anyway. I have something to tell you too. You remember that guy you met at Fox Creek—Jeremiah?"

"Yeah, what about him?"

"I saw him in the woods. He lives there with his brother and sister. They ran away from a ranch."

"Why'd they do that?"

Spike told Logan the whole story. "He's the one who stole the food from the senior center. He admitted it. He said he couldn't stand to see his brother and sister crying because they were hungry."

"Are you going to turn him in?"

"I promised I wouldn't. That's one promise I'm gonna keep!"

Beth Anne stood at the door of the Bluesky Bowling Center to greet her friends as they arrived at her birthday party. She was wearing a new capri outfit. "Wow! Look at you!" Melissa exclaimed, checking Beth Anne out from head to toe.

"My grandma gave me a makeover for my birthday," Beth Anne said proudly. "See my nails, and I got my hair cut and styled."

"You look very nice," Laura and Amber agreed. "A lot better than *our* makeover," Laura said, laughing.

Beth Anne had invited the Handy Helpers and everyone on the Special Olympics swim team. Lisa ushered the party guests to the counter to get their bowling shoes, except for Joey, who wouldn't need shoes because he was in a wheelchair.

"How is Joey going to bowl?" Melissa asked Brianna.

"He uses a ramp," Brianna told her. "He sets the ball on top of the ramp and then pushes it so it goes down the ramp and down the alley. You'll see, Joey's a good bowler."

The lanes had already been assigned and names entered in the computer. As soon as the guests found a bowling ball that fit their fingers, they were ready to start bowling. Beth Anne had bowled in Special Olympics the year before. She had developed her own style—pushing the ball between her legs.

"Somehow it works." Lisa laughed as everyone watched Beth Anne's ball go down the alley in what seemed like slow motion. Just before the rack came down, her ball knocked over seven pins.

Spike surprised everyone with his professional-looking bowling style. "I bowl on a junior league," he said.

"You have to be on my bowling team!" Beth Anne insisted.

"Are you sure you want me on your team?" Spike asked.

"I'm sure she won't take no for an answer," Kevin, Beth Anne's father, said with a laugh.

Shelly had never bowled before. She tried doing it like Beth Anne, but her ball kept going in the gutter. Spike tried to help her by guiding the ball and telling her when to let it go. But that didn't really help. Her score for one entire game was eight.

"Why don't you try using the ramp?" Brianna suggested.

Spike picked up the strange apparatus with two straight legs and two long curved legs. He lined the curved legs up with the foul line and placed the ball at the top of the ramp. Shelly gave it a good push. The ball went straight down the middle for a split. "I got eight!" she shouted. "I got eight with one ball!"

Spike was the big winner of the day with a score of 135 and 117. Everyone congratulated him, and Lisa presented him with a little plastic trophy.

Cake and ice cream followed the bowling. Then the birthday girl opened her presents. She got Barbies and Barbie stuff from most of her friends. Her parents gave her a new swimsuit. They also gave her the motor home she asked for so her Barbies could go on vacation to Disneyland.

As they were leaving, the Handy Helpers gathered around Spike.

"I miss you guys." Spike tried to smile.

"We really miss you," Laura said.

"Sorry you have to spend the summer working," Chris added.

"Don't worry about me. Gus is a good guy, and working on the trail is kinda fun. I'm doing fine, really."

Todd's Bronco was parked in the driveway when Spike got home. "That's all I need." he sighed.

"Hi, bro." Todd grabbed him around the shoulders and rubbed his knuckles in Spike's hair. Spike struggled to get away.

"Better not mess with the do," Jennifer warned.

"Oh, yeah, *Spike*," Todd teased. "I forgot. Your hair's your trademark."

"That's right," Spike said. "I don't like people messing with my hair."

Before letting him go, Todd tussled Spike's hair one more time.

It seemed like a dark monsoon cloud was hanging over the Handy Helpers as they held their Monday afternoon meeting. Logan informed them that Spike was not going to be a volunteer at the senior center anymore. "He can still help with outside jobs," Logan explained, "and we'll keep him in the phone circle in case of emergencies."

"Maybe after he finishes his community service, the board will reconsider," Walt said, looking around at the sad faces. "We'll just have to wait and see."

The Handy Helpers were about to leave when Walt called Amber over. "Can you give this to your dad? It's the nanny cam he loaned me to put out back so we could try to catch the thief. It's been out there several days. I'm sure whoever stole that food is long gone."

"Sure," Amber said, "I'll give it to my dad."

"What's that?" Logan asked as everyone was getting on their bikes.

"It's a nanny cam Walt was using to catch the thief. I have to give it back to my dad."

"Do you have to give it to him right away?" Logan asked.

"What do you have in mind?" Chris looked at him curiously.

"There's not much we can do to help Spike except maybe show his parents what Todd's really like. If they know what's been going on, they'll understand why Spike did what he did."

"Spying on someone else's house with a camera is against the law, isn't it?" Laura asked, worried.

"You're probably right," Logan said. "I guess it's a bad idea."

"Why don't you give the nanny cam to Spike and let him set it up?" Chris suggested. "It's not against the law to bug your own house, is it?"

CHAPTER THIRTEEN

It was a spark of lightning that started the fire. Citizens all over Bluesky heard the loud crack of thunder, and if they were looking out their windows, they saw the lightning streak across the sky as a dramatic flash of white. It would be several hours before the forest ranger sitting in the tower on the top of Granger Mountain using binoculars would spot the blaze. By that time, it would have burned over a hundred acres. It would be the next morning before firefighters reached the flames that were now raging out of control through the underbrush and threatening the tall ponderosa pines. Spike smelled the smoke as he and Gus hiked the trail to their worksite. "Don't worry," Gus assured him. "The fire's burning away from us. We're not in any danger here."

Gus was correct in saying the fire was burning in the opposite direction. It was burning away from their worksite but toward a community of forest homes called Pinecone Ranch. A shelter had been set up in the Bluesky High School gym, and homeowners in the path of the fire were being evacuated. The senior center had been called upon to help distribute food and water to the residents of the shelter. Logan had started the phone circle by calling Chris. "You'll have to skip Spike," he said sadly, "and call Laura. She's the next one on the phone circle."

"Okay," Chris said. "I'll see you at the high school at ten o'clock."

The Handy Helpers spent the day at the shelter, helping families get settled. The police department sent over a big bag of stuffed animals. "Little kids don't really understand what's going on," Officer Fillmore explained. "Having a stuffed animal is comforting and gives them something that's just theirs."

Cases of bottled water, food, clothing, and bedding were being dropped off constantly. Chris and Logan helped move the supplies to the staging area. Meals had to be prepared and served. The girls leant a hand with the food. Melissa and Laura joined the serving line, dishing out mashed potatoes or handing out rolls. Beth Anne and Amber helped people in the dining area and cleared the tables when they were through eating.

In between helping with meals, the Handy Helpers spent time talking to the families in the shelter. Beth Anne handed a fluffy white stuffed cat to a little girl about two years old with her thumb in her mouth. She was trying to hide behind her mother. "Look, Sissy," her mother said sweetly. "Isn't it a soft, pretty kitty this little girl has for you?"

Sissy took the cat from Beth Anne with her spare hand and then tucked herself farther behind her mother. "She knows something's wrong. I tried to pretend we were on vacation, but she knows the difference."

An elderly couple were seated together on some folding chairs. The man had his arm around his wife who had tears in her eyes. "Can we do anything for you?" Chris asked.

"No, we're fine," the man said. "My wife's pretty worried. Everything we have is in that house, all our pictures and memories. I don't know what we'll do if it burns down."

All day long, the Handy Helpers heard stories like that from the people in the shelter.

"I wish there was more we could do," Laura said.

"Just being here is a lot," Walt told them. "This may be the worst thing these families have ever had to face. It helps them to know that someone cares."

The workers on the Rancho Vista trail could hear the planes overhead as they flew to Pine Lake to scoop up water. The slurry the planes had dumped on the fire caused an eerie red glow in the eastern sky, making the fire seem closer than it really was. Spike was hoping for a chance to see if Jeremiah was still at his lean-to. He thought they had probably moved on with the fire so close, but he wanted to see for himself.

The opportunity came just after the crew had finished their lunch break. Bert was working on a particularly steep part of the trail above the ravine. He had laid his shovel down to collect some weeds he had dug up. One weed must have still been rooted in the ground. As Bert tugged on it, trying to pull it up, he lost his footing. His boot hit his shovel, propelling it down into the ravine. "I can get it for you," Spike offered. "I'll have to go around and come up from the other side. It might take awhile, but I know I can get there."

"Go ahead then," Terry told him. "We don't want to leave a shovel out here in the forest."

Grabbing his backpack, Spike made his way down the ravine as he had done several times before. Slowly picking his way up the dry creek bed, he kept his eye on the bright crimson sky. "Seeing that," he said to himself, "I bet Jeremiah's moved out. He's probably long gone."

To Spike's surprise, he saw Jeremiah walking toward him as he approached the lean-to. "I didn't expect to see you here," Spike said. "I figured the fire would drive you out."

"The fire's burning away from us," Jeremiah said. "I decided we were safer here than trying to move somewhere else. Besides, there've been so many trucks and forest rangers in the area I was afraid we'd get caught trying to leave."

"You should be safe here," Spike said. "I brought you some more food. My mom's noticed things missing, so I was afraid to take too much. My friends pitched in and helped with stuff from their kitchens. Maybe it'll keep you going until the fire's out."

"Thanks," Jeremiah said. "You've been a good friend."

Rachel took Spike by the hand and showed him the rocks she had collected outside their lean-to. "I think this might have gold in it," she said, showing him a white rock with black veins and some gold flecks.

"You might be right." Spike gave Rachel a friendly smile. "That's white quartz. It could have gold in it."

"I can use my gold to buy us a house," Rachel sounded serious.

"I think it would take a lot of gold to buy a house," Spike told her.

While they were looking at the rocks, Daniel came up behind them. Occasionally a squeaking sound came from him. "Hi, Daniel," Spike said without looking up. "How are you today?"

"There's a . . . there's a fire," Daniel said.

"Yes, I know." Spike smiled at him. "But you don't have to worry. It's burning away from you. You're safe here."

Spike made his way back up the dry creek bed until he was just below the area where the crew was working. He located Bert's shovel and picked it up. "Hey, up there!" he called out. Gus looked down over the edge of the ravine. "You made it!" he called down to Spike. "Come on back. We're about to quit for the day."

"This is the last day we'll be working on the trail for a while," Terry told the work crew as they hiked out. "I got a call from Sam at the ranger station. The fire's under control enough that we're starting on the cleanup."

"Can we help with the cleanup?" Spike asked.

"I'm afraid not," Terry told him. "We can't let civilians into that area. It's too dangerous. There are still burning embers that could ignite at any time, and the forest could be blazing again."

"What about my community service?" Spike asked Gus as they rode back to town. "I've got six hours left. I don't want the judge to get mad and throw me in jail."

"That won't happen," Gus assured him. "There's nothing you can do under the circumstances. The judge'll understand."

"Mom!" Jennifer yelled. "Didn't you buy any bread yesterday?"

"Yes, there's a loaf in the bread box."

"No there's not. And there's no peanut butter or granola bars. Where's all the food going?"

Spike, who was just about to enter the kitchen when he overheard their conversation, turned and walked back toward his bedroom.

"Just a minute, young man!" his mother called after him. "You come right back here!"

"What's up?" Spike asked innocently.

"Food has been disappearing from our kitchen all week. I want you to tell me why."

"What makes you think I'd know anything about it? I've been working on the trail all week. Why don't you ask Monica? She's been home. Maybe she's bulking up for softball."

"Not likely," Carolyn said. "If any more food turns up missing, it's coming out of *your* allowance. Those guys you're working with on the trail can buy their own food!"

Spike was surprised when he called Logan to see if he wanted to go fishing at Fox Creek. Logan's mom told him that Logan was at the high school helping the people staying in the shelter. "Maybe I can help them too," Spike said. "I'll go see what's up."

Riding his bike to the high school, Spike wondered what it would be like to leave all your possessions behind and go to a shelter. The families wouldn't know if they would even have a home to go back to. *The kids in those families must be really scared,* Spike thought. Then he remembered the little family hiding in the forest. *About as scared as Rachel and Daniel.*

"Hi," Spike called out to Walt as he rode up to the high school gym. "I'm here to help."

"Sorry," Walt said sadly. "I can't let you stay. The Handy Helpers are here as volunteers from the senior center."

"That's okay." Spike hung his head. "Don't sweat it."

Just as Spike was getting on his bike to leave, Logan called out his name. "Walt said I can't help!" Spike yelled back at Logan. "I'm gonna go home!"

"Wait a minute!" Logan called out.

Spike straddled his bike and waited in the parking lot. "How's the work going?" Logan asked.

"It's okay. We can't work on the trail right now 'cause Frank and Terry have to help clean up from the fire."

"Are you having any more problems with Todd?"

"A little, but I'm handling it."

"What if your parents knew the truth about Todd? Would that help?"

"I guess so, but Todd's got them snowed."

"Meet us at the park at two. I think we have a way to fix things."

A loud cheer was coming from the crowd in the gym as Logan returned. "What's going on?" he asked Amber.

"Just listen," Amber said, pointing to the large television screen that had been set up at one end of the gym.

"The fire is sixty percent contained," the announcer was saying. "The fire breaks are holding, and it's no longer threatening the homes in Pinecone Ranch. The residents should be able to return home soon."

"That's really great news!" Logan joined in with the cheers.

Spike went to the park early, anxious to have time to spend with his friends. He was surprised to see that no one was there. Maybe it was the hot, muggy weather or the threat of rain or worry about the forest fire, but for whatever reason, the park was empty.

The Handy Helpers came riding up on their bikes, everyone except Beth Anne, whose mother had taken her home.

"It's nice to see you guys," Spike said.

"It's great to see you," everyone told him. "It's just not the same without you," Laura added.

"Thanks." Spike tried to smile.

"The reason I asked you to meet us here is so we can tell you about our plan," Logan began. "It has to do with this nanny cam. Amber's dad loaned it to Walt so he could catch the guy who stole the food at the senior center."

"Did they catch him?" Spike asked, worried.

"No," Logan went on, pretending he didn't know why Spike was concerned. "They're sure whoever did it left town a long time ago. Anyway, Walt asked Amber to return the nanny cam. But we thought that maybe you could set it up some place where you could catch Todd being a bully. Then you can show your family the video. That way they'll have to see that you've been telling the truth about him."

"Yeah," Spike said. "It might work. But I'm not sure where to put it."

"Why don't you put it on your front porch?" Laura suggested.

"That's a good idea." Spike nodded. "Jennifer usually goes in the house, and Todd hangs out in front and gives me a hard time."

"It's worth a try anyway," Amber added. "What do you have to lose?"

"Nothing, I guess. Thanks, guys. I'm glad I have friends like you."

Amber showed Spike how to use the nanny cam. "You see how small it is? You can hide it anywhere. This is how you turn it on. When you're ready to see what you've captured, you can hook it up to your computer using this cable."

"That sounds easy enough," Spike said. "I'll set it up as soon as I get home."

Riding home on his bike, Spike noticed the wind suddenly begin to stir. In the east, the sky was a dirty-brown color instead of the usual blue. "There's a dust storm rolling in," Spike said. "That must be why no one was at the park." He pushed harder on the pedals and propelled his bike forward at a faster pace. "I sure hope I can beat the storm to my house!"

Spike saw Todd's Bronco parked in the driveway when he got home. "Better watch out, Todd," he said to himself. "You're about to get caught on camera." He took the nanny cam out of his pocket and looked for a good location on the front porch. Spike considered putting it in one of the planters but was afraid that it might get ruined if someone watered the plants. Then he noticed the wreath his mother had made out of dried flowers and colorful ribbons. She had hung it securely on the front door. "Perfect," Spike said as he pushed the nanny cam in place within the wreath. "No one will ever notice it there."

Todd was alone in the family room when Spike came through the door. "Where's Jennifer?" Spike asked.

"She's changing her clothes. You know how women are. They can take hours."

Spike took a seat in a chair near the sofa where Todd was sitting. They were quiet for a time, and then Spike asked, "I've been wondering, Todd . . . I've been thinking . . . You're gonna be a senior next year. What are your plans?"

"What do you care?"

"I just thought . . . I mean, someday I'll be a senior, and I just wondered what it's like to be done with school."

"Well, for one thing, everybody keeps asking you what your plans are. And if you don't really know, it gets annoying!"

"Sorry I asked!" Spike turned on the television and began surfing the channels.

"Actually I do have something I'd like to do," Todd said after a few minutes.

"What is it?"

"I don't usually tell anyone because I'm afraid they'll laugh."

"I promise I won't laugh. What is it?"

"I like to take pictures. I'd like to be a photographer."

"What's wrong with that? If that's what you like to do, you should do it."

"But what if I'm not good enough? What if I can't make any money taking pictures?"

"You still should do what you like. Who said you aren't good enough?"

"I took some pictures at the river, but Jennifer didn't like the pictures of her. She told me to erase them, but I didn't. That's why she got mad at me."

"Can I see them?"

"Sure." Todd showed him a picture of Jennifer on an inner tube, floating down the river. Her head was back, and she was laughing as she kicked water in the air.

"What's wrong with that?" Spike asked.

"She said her hair was a mess and her face looked funny."

"That's a great picture! I think you should keep it."

"Thanks, I will."

"You two seem to be getting along better," Jennifer said as she walked into the family room.

"Sure," Todd replied confidently, "I told you we're bros."

Jennifer sat next to Todd on the sofa. "Let me have the remote," she said to Spike. Jennifer cruised through the channels until something caught everyone's attention. It was breaking news about the forest fire.

"This just in," the reporter said. "The ranch fire that was almost seventy percent contained has been stirred to life by the wind storm that is blowing in from the southeast. The fire has now changed course and is burning toward the nearby campgrounds. Any campers left in the Pine Lake area are being evacuated by the forest service. The entire area is being closed off. Barricades have been set up on the main road as well as forest service roads. Residents are asked to observe the barricades and stay out of the area."

Spike took the phone into his room and called information to get the phone number for the ranger station. When someone answered the phone, he asked to speak to Frank or Terry. "Are you evacuating the campgrounds?" Spike asked Terry. "There are three kids living in the forest. They have a little shelter just above the dry creek bed. I saw them there yesterday. I promised I wouldn't tell anyone, but now I have to. They could be in danger."

CHAPTER FOURTEEN

"Let's meet at the park," Logan said to Chris on the phone. "Then we can figure out what to do."

"Did Spike try telling the police?" Chris asked.

"He's tried everybody—the police, the forest service, Gus, his parents."

"No one will believe him?"

"I think they believe him, but they keep saying everybody's been evacuated."

As agreed, the boys met at the swings in the park. Spike had a look of panic on his face like Logan and Chris had never seen before, not even when he thought he was going to jail.

"I've tried everyone," Spike said. "Everybody keeps telling me the same thing. The forest rangers drove and hiked through that whole area. There are no campers left. They've all been evacuated."

"Maybe Jeremiah left after the fire changed direction," Logan said. "What makes you think he would stay there?"

"The last day I worked on the trail, Jeremiah told me they were going to stay put. He was worried about all the forest trucks driving around. He might not know the fire changed direction. I have to make sure. If they're still there, I'm their only hope."

"We'll never make it there on our bikes," Chris pointed out. "It's too far. It would be dark before we got there, and we might get lost. We need somebody with a car."

"Gus was our last chance, and he said no," Logan reminded them. "There's nobody else."

"There *is* one more person with a car," Spike said, hesitantly, "but I hate to ask him."

"Todd!" Chris and Logan shouted together.

"You have to ask him!" Chris said forcefully. "You have no choice!"

Chris and Logan waited as Spike knocked on Todd's door. Spike insisted on asking him by himself. "It's time I stood up to Todd. I've gotta make him understand how important this is."

"We're leaving in an hour," Spike told his friends waiting at the curb. "Todd's gonna ask Andy and Chase to go with us. He said to wear jeans and sturdy shoes. Bring some water and a flashlight. Also, if you can get a blanket, Todd thought that would be a good idea just in case."

"In case of what?" Chris asked.

"I don't know," Spike admitted. "I didn't ask."

Todd's Bronco pulled up in the parking lot at the park at four o'clock as planned. Andy got out to let Chris and Logan into the backseat with Chase. Spike slid across the front seat next to Todd. "Where are we going?" Todd asked Spike.

"You know the road to Pine Lake? That's where we're going."

Smoke from the fire combined with dust stirred up by the monsoon winds hung over the valley, blocking out the sun, making it seem much later than it was. Soon the roads into the forest would be closed off. There was only a slim chance that they could get there in time. But no one was willing to admit that they might already be too late.

Todd turned onto the main road leading up the mountain. As they feared, all the gates were closed to the forest roads, and the dirt roads with no gates had barricades. Forest rangers had been posted at the barricades to make sure no one got into the area. Finally, the boys reached the parking lot for the Rancho Vista Trail. To their dismay, it was full of forest vehicles and rangers.

"Do you have a plan B?" Todd asked Spike.

"No, I was hoping this trail would still be open."

"Didn't you say this trail was going to meet up with the Sidewinder Trail?" Logan asked.

"It's supposed to, but that's over two miles away, and the trail's not finished." Spike was starting to panic.

"I've hiked in that area with my scout troop," Logan continued. "I think I know a way in. We'll have a longer hike, maybe four miles, but we should be able to get there, hopefully before dark."

Todd followed the directions Logan gave him. To their relief there were no other cars on the dirt road leading to the Sidewinder trailhead. "All the forest rangers are busy on the Pine Lake road. It looks like we're in the clear," Todd said.

"Good thing you have four-wheel drive," Logan pointed out. "We're gonna need it on this road!"

It was an old jeep road used by a rancher who had cattle grazing in a meadow several miles in. The road was not maintained at all but was full of deep ruts and boulders. Todd did his best to miss as many obstacles as possible, but the boys in the back were struggling to sit up straight. "Guess I should have worn my spurs." Chris laughed.

At last, Logan told Todd to pull over. Ahead they could see a marker for the Sidewinder Trail. "We should be able to hike in from here."

"We have about two hours of daylight left," Andy pointed out. "We're gonna have to hike fast to get there before dark!"

"At least, we have a chance." Spike sighed. "That's more than we had a few hours ago."

The trail was fairly flat as it wove through an area of manzanita and shaggy-bark juniper, crossing a dry creek bed several times. The hikers turned around often to check the location of the sun as it made its decent down the western sky. Each time they quickened their pace in the race against the declining sunlight.

The smoke from the fire was settling into the small canyon where they were hiking. Chris began coughing and was soon joined by Chase, who seemed to be having trouble breathing. "I have asthma," Chase admitted. "This smoke is really bothering me."

"Maybe you should go back," Andy suggested.

"No, I want to keep going. I have my inhaler if I need it."

At last, the trail began to lead them out of the canyon. It was gradual at first but then became steeper as the hikers made their way toward a rocky saddle covered with scraggly pine trees. "How much farther do you think it is?" Todd asked Logan.

"The Sidewinder Trail goes about three miles before it meets the Crown Trail that goes to the top of the mountain. I'm thinking that if we turn right instead of left, we should be headed toward the Rancho Vista Trail."

"What if we get lost?" Andy asked. "We could wander around out here all night."

"I've spent a lot of time in that area the last few weeks," Spike said, trying to sound confident. "I'm pretty sure I can find my way to the ravine."

The sun dropped behind the hill as the hikers reached the junction with the Crown Trail. "Anything look familiar?" Todd asked Spike.

"No, not yet. I think we should go that way." Spike pointed toward a clearing he could see between the pine trees. "That seems like the right direction to me."

Spike kept watching for the ravine. He knew it would look different from this side. If he missed it, they might never find Jeremiah's camp. The remaining glimmer of sunlight was fading fast now, but the hikers decided to save their flashlights until it was totally dark. Without a trail to follow, they were forced to slow their pace to find the easiest way around the brush and thickets. They reached the top of a hill and started over the other side. Descending slowly at first, the slope of the hill became steeper until the hikers were struggling to keep from sliding down into the dark abyss below. Suddenly they found themselves at the edge of a cliff.

"What should we do now?" Todd asked as he shined his flashlight down into the creek bed. "It looks like we've reached a dead end."

"This is it!" Spike yelled, excited. "This is the ravine! Look!" He shined his flashlight across the ravine and up the other side. There was just enough sunlight left to help light up the end of the Rancho Vista Trail.

"How are we going to get down there?" Chris asked. "It looks too steep."

Spike led the group to the left along the cliff until they reached a place where it was possible to climb down into the ravine. From there, he was able to find the trail he had used before. The large boulders in the dry creek bed made hiking difficult, but Spike was determined to get through. At last, he led his fellow hikers to the clearing on the other side. Just as they were passing a clump of bushes, they heard a squeaking sound. "Must be a mouse worried about the fire," Chris said. "He really sounds scared."

"Shhh." Spike put his finger up to his lips. There was no sound, and then the squeaking started again.

"Daniel!" Spike called out. "Daniel, don't be afraid. It's me, Michael. We're here to rescue you."

After a few minutes, a boy crawled out of the brush. Todd shined his flashlight in the boy's direction. He was shaking dead leaves and grass from his pants, and his face seemed to be twitching.

"It's okay," Spike said soothingly. "You're safe. No one will hurt you."

"Help Rachel," Daniel said. "Can you help Rachel?"

"Where's Jeremiah?" Spike asked.

"Gone . . . He's gone to town," Daniel looked like he was going to cry.

"Where's Rachel?"

"Up there." Daniel pointed toward the trees where the lean-to stood.

Spike led the way up through the trees until they were all standing outside the lean-to.

"Rachel!" Spike called out.

Moaning came from inside the lean-to. Spike shined his flashlight inside where he saw Rachel huddled in a corner on the pine-needle bed. "Are you okay?" he asked.

"I'm scared," she cried. "The fire is coming! We're all gonna get burned up!"

"That's why we're here," Spike said softly. "We're going to get you out of here."

Spike told Daniel to go inside the lean-to with Rachel. Then he joined his friends nearby. "I don't think Rachel and Daniel can make it back the way we came. It's too far for them to hike."

"We could take turns carrying them," Todd suggested.

"But we have that big climb to get out of the ravine," Spike reminded him.

"So what are you thinking?" Logan asked.

"What if some of us hike out the Rancho Vista Trail with Daniel and Rachel? It's a lot shorter, and the forest rangers are there. They'll help us get back to town. The rest of you can go back on the Sidewinder Trail to Todd's Bronco."

"That's not a bad plan," Andy said. "I'll go with Michael, and you guys can go back with Todd."

"I'll go along with you," Chase offered. "I can help with Rachel and Daniel."

"Are you sure, Chase?" Todd asked. "What about your asthma?"

"I'll use my inhaler. I'll be okay. Besides, the sooner I get out of this smoke, the better."

"Your parents must be worried by now," Todd said to Spike.

"I hadn't thought about that," Spike admitted. "I'll probably be grounded for life!"

"Me too," Logan and Chris added.

"As soon as I can get reception on my phone," Todd promised, "I'll call and let your parents know you're okay."

"Let's go," Spike poked his head in the door of the lean-to. "We're getting out of here."

"Wait!" Rachel shouted. "I have to get something."

"What's that?" Spike asked as she dug in the dirt in a corner of the lean-to.

"It's my gold," Rachel said. "I need my gold to buy a house."

Spike led the way back through the dry creek bed. Once they reached the edge of the ravine, the two groups parted.

"Stay safe, bro," Todd said.

"You too," Spike added. "See you back in town."

Andy and Chase helped Rachel and Daniel make their way out of the ravine. Soon they were walking on the completed part of the Rancho Vista Trail. They stopped and gave the kids drinks of water. "Don't worry," Andy said. "Everything will be okay."

Over the ridge, a bright-red glow was visible in the night sky. As the hikers reached the top of the ridge, they could see flames as the trees below them were burning. Rachel started to cry. "The fire's gonna get us!"

Andy picked her up, and she buried her face in his shoulder. "Don't worry. The fire is a lot farther away than it looks."

As they hiked closer to the fire, the smoke was overwhelming. Chase was struggling to breathe. "Use the blanket you're carrying to cover your head," Andy suggested. "That'll help protect you from the smoke." Andy threw his blanket over Rachel, who was coughing. After a while, Andy felt her body go limp. He was hoping she had fallen asleep.

Daniel stumbled a little as he followed Spike through the switchbacks leading down the other side of the mountain. If his calculations were correct, Spike knew they had about a mile to go. A terrifying thought entered his mind—what if the rangers had pulled out already?

The night was quiet. *Animals are smart enough not to stick around when there's a fire.* Spike thought. Worried the pace was too fast, he stopped and offered Daniel another drink of water. Andy took the opportunity to ask Chase to check on Rachel. "She's sleeping," Chase assured him. "That's probably the best thing."

The blanket over Chase's head was helping a little, but he was wheezing badly. "Are you all right?" Spike asked him between coughing spells.

"Yeah, but let's get out of here as fast as we can."

Spike pressed on with Daniel close on his heels. On both sides of the trail, the ponderosa pines stood as sentries of the forest. A feeling of sadness came over Spike as he thought what it would be like if the fire burned along the trail. Having worked on it, he felt a sort of ownership in it. It would be like losing a good friend.

As the hikers left the pine trees behind and entered the area with chaparral, the trail leveled off. Spike knew they were nearing the trailhead, and his fears returned. Suddenly, truck lights were shining in their faces, and men were yelling "What are you doing there?" "Are you all right?"

The rangers had watched the lights from the flashlights coming down the trail. As the hikers came closer, they had moved a truck in position to light the way. Now they were running toward the hikers. One of them took Rachel and carried her to the truck. Spike recognized Frank and Terry among the rangers. He gave them a weak smile. "Glad to see you guys," he said.

"Well, we weren't expecting to see you!" Terry exclaimed. "What are you doing out here?"

"We had to save Rachel and Daniel," Spike tried to explain. "No one would believe they were out here in the forest, so we had to rescue them ourselves."

"How did you get in here without being seen?" Frank asked.

"On the Sidewinder Trail," Spike said. "But we didn't think Rachel and Daniel could make it out that way. I'm sure glad you guys are still here."

Chase was coughing harder and having trouble breathing. "We have oxygen on the truck," Terry said. "We'll fix you up."

Spike felt exhausted as he rode back to town in the forest service truck. The lights from homes in Pinecone Ranch were visible in the distance. "I guess some families got to go back home," he said. "At least, it worked out for them."

"We're all safe," Chase pointed out. "Everything's gonna be fine."

"I hope my parents see it that way," Spike said, his voice shaking.

"What are you going to do with Rachel and Daniel?" Spike asked the rangers as they drove into Bluesky.

"I guess we'll take them to the shelter," Terry said. "There are still some people there. Or we can take them to the police station."

Spike thought for a moment. "The shelter would be better than the police station. They're already scared. No reason to scare them anymore."

It was ten o'clock when Terry pulled the forest service truck up in front of the high school gym. "We can walk home from here," Andy said. Spike thanked them for their help and then followed Frank and Terry to the gym. The door was locked, but Frank quickly found the security guard who opened it for him. Half of the families had been allowed back into their homes. The remaining families were sleeping on cots in the dark gym.

Once his eyes adjusted to the darkness, Spike looked around the gym for a familiar face.

Snoring was coming from a nearby cot. The dim light was enough to shine on a bald head that Spike recognized as Gus. "I was too tired to go home," Gus admitted when Spike shook him awake. "What are you doing here?"

"This is Daniel and Rachel," Spike explained. "They're the kids I told you about who live in the forest. Todd helped us rescue them. Now they need somewhere to stay."

Gus quickly located two empty cots. Terry laid the sleeping Rachel on a cot. Daniel lay down on a cot near her.

"Can we give you a ride home?" Terry asked Spike.

"I left my bike at the park," Spike said. "But I guess I can get it tomorrow."

Spike had prepared himself for a loud reception at home, but his parents were surprisingly calm.

"Todd called and told us what happened," Carolyn said to her son. "We're relieved that you're okay."

"Aren't you mad at me?" Spike asked.

"It's late," his dad said. "Go on to bed now, and we'll talk about it in the morning."

CHAPTER FIFTEEN

It was almost nine o'clock the next morning when Spike opened his eyes. He couldn't believe his mom had let him sleep that late. He dressed quickly and headed to the kitchen for food to quiet his rumbling stomach.

"Well," his mom said, "look who finally decided to make an appearance."

"You didn't wake me up," Spike said, rubbing his eyes.

"I thought you needed the sleep. Fix something to eat, and then come in the family room. Your dad and I want to have a talk with you."

Here it comes, Spike thought, *the big lecture*. He took out two eggs and scrambled them in a bowl before pouring them into a small skillet. Then he put some bread into the toaster.

When he had finished eating his breakfast, Spike walked hesitantly into the family room where his dad was reading the newspaper and his mother was looking at e-mails.

"What are your plans for today?" David asked his son.

"I want to go to the shelter and check on Rachel and Daniel. They're probably scared without their brother. I want to make sure they're all right."

"Your dad and I had a long talk last night, and we feel we owe you an apology," Carolyn said, turning off the computer.

"You do?" Spike sounded confused.

"We haven't done a very good job of listening to you lately," David began. "If we had, you wouldn't have felt like you had to rescue those kids. Of course that doesn't get you off the hook for pulling a stunt like that. You could have all been killed in the fire!"

"I know," Spike said with a sigh. "We were really lucky."

"Not to mention scaring your parents half to death," Carolyn added. "We had no idea where you were until Todd called."

"I'm sorry. I won't do anything like that again."

"If you have a problem, son," David said, putting his hands on Spike's shoulders, "you can always come to us. We're going to do a lot better job listening in the future."

"We should have taken you seriously," Carolyn added. "It's just that you're always playing those pranks on everybody. We're never sure what to believe."

"Yeah," Spike sighed. "I guess it's like that boy who cried wolf as a joke and then when the wolf came for real, no one believed him."

"That's exactly right," Carolyn said. "When you started telling us about Todd, we didn't believe you. But now we know that was true."

"How do you know that?" Spike was confused again.

"Todd came by and talked to us this morning," Carolyn explained. "He told us everything, about the name-calling and the dirty dishes—everything."

"I'm sorry, son," David put his hand on Spike's shoulder. "I really let you down."

"That's okay, Dad. I shouldn't have played all those pranks. I'm giving that up for good!"

"That's nice to hear." Carolyn smiled. "But we might miss them a little. Some of your stunts were really funny."

Spike walked to the park where he found his bike still locked in the bike rack. Then he rode to the high school. "They're not here," he was told by one of the men staying in the shelter. "This bigger boy showed up, and I think Gus took them to his house."

As fast as he could, Spike rode his bike to Gus's. When he knocked on the door, Jeremiah answered. "Hi, Michael," he said.

"How did you get here?" Spike asked once he was seated in Gus's living room.

"Todd picked me up in his Bronco," Jeremiah explained. "I was walking back from town when Logan recognized me and made Todd stop. They told us you were taking Daniel and Rachel to the forest rangers. When we got to the shelter, Daniel and Rachel were there with Gus. We all spent the night at the shelter, and then Gus brought us here this morning."

"I'm sorry I broke my promise," Spike said sadly.

"I'm glad you did," Jeremiah replied. "I'm not sure I could have gotten to Rachel and Daniel in time. You probably saved their lives."

"But now they're going to put you in foster homes and maybe split you up." Spike continued to be concerned.

"At least, we're alive," Jeremiah went on. "Gus said we can stay here for awhile. We'll just wait and see what happens with the authorities."

Rachel and Daniel had been sitting on the floor in front of the television. Rachel got up and took Spike's hand. She led him to a spot on the floor next to Daniel.

"They haven't seen a television for a long time." Jeremiah laughed. "They have lots of catching up to do."

Spike was sitting on the floor with Rachel and Daniel when Gus came through the front door carrying groceries. "Hi," he said to Spike. "I forgot how much food kids can eat. I had to make a grocery run."

"Thanks for helping," Spike said. "I'm glad they didn't have to stay in the shelter."

"I should be apologizing to you. You tried to tell me about the kids, and I didn't take you seriously. If I had, I could have done more to help sooner."

"At least, it turned out okay," Spike pointed out. "So far anyway. I guess we'll have to wait and see what happens."

"Don't worry about that now," Gus said. "I've got a pretty good idea that everything is gonna work out fine."

Spike was on his computer when Chris and Logan came to visit. "How are you feeling today?" Logan asked.

"A little tired. How about you?"

"I'm kind of tired too, but I'm glad everything worked out okay."

"Did you talk to Gus today?" Chris asked.

"I went over to his house. Jeremiah was there. He told me how you found him walking on the road and picked him up."

"He sure was happy when we got to the shelter and his brother and sister were there," Chris said. "What do you think will happen to them now?"

"I don't know," Spike said. "But I know Gus will do whatever he can to help them."

"Todd turned out to be a pretty good guy in the end," Logan pointed out. "He got us all back to the Bronco and took us home."

"I guess I was wrong about him," Spike admitted. "Maybe he *was* just trying to treat me like a little brother. This morning he told my parents everything that's been going on between us. I couldn't believe it!"

"When the going gets tough," Chris said, "you really find out who your friends are."

"I suppose I won't be needing that nanny cam." Spike kind of laughed. "I'll just give it back to Amber."

"Don't you want to look at the video first?" Chris said. "There might be some funny stuff on it."

"Like what?" Spike gave him a curious look.

"Like Todd and Jennifer for example." Chris grinned.

"Yuck! I really don't wanna see that!" Spike stuck his finger in his mouth, pretending to gag.

"You really should check it out and make sure it's all erased before you give it to Amber," Logan suggested.

"Okay," Spike groaned. "I'll get it, and we can connect it to my computer. But if it has Jennifer and Todd making out, I'm not looking!"

The boys had been playing the video for almost an hour, fast-forwarding through the parts with no people. They watched as Jennifer and Todd walked to the front door. Todd kissed Jennifer good night, but it was definitely a G-rated kiss.

"Well, I expected something better than that!" Spike said, disappointed. "I didn't get any good stuff."

"Wait a minute," Chris said when they resumed the fast-forward. "Go back. I think we missed something."

"That's my dad!" Spike stared at the computer screen, watching his dad walk out the front door. "What's that in his hand? It's a bowl. He's eating cereal. No wonder we always run out. I bet he sneaks out every night!"

"What are you going to do?" Logan asked. "You can't tell him you've been spying on him."

"No, I think I'll keep this as our little secret. Mom and my sisters are always whispering about something they call girl stuff. This can be guy stuff."

Spike sat on the edge of his bed, thinking about what he had to do. It had been three days since the rescue on Granger Mountain. Jeremiah, Rachel, and Daniel were safe. Everything seemed to be working out fine. Spike just had one thing to take care of.

From the back of his closet, he pulled out a box. Opening it, he took out the contents one item at a time. There was the half-melted ice cream bar he took with him to the movie theater. It seemed like some tall person always sat in front of him. He put the fake ice cream bar on the seat so no one would sit there. Next he took out rubber dog poo. Once he put that on Jennifer's bed. She banned Tigger from her room for a week. There was the fake barf he bought thinking he could use it to get out of doing something, like going to school. Unfortunately, his mom wasn't fooled by it at all. "It doesn't smell like throw-up," she had said. In the bottom of the box was his toy rat. "Chuck. I can't get rid of you! I think it would be okay to keep just one thing from my gag box."

Spike found a safe place for Chuck on his bookshelf. Then he carried the box outside and waited at the curb. A few minutes later, Gus pulled up.

"Can we make one stop on our way?" Spike asked. "I'm donating this stuff to the thrift store."

Gus waited in the truck as Spike carried his box into the Community Thrift Shop. Just as he was handing the box to the thrift shop worker, he noticed the whoopee cushion. It was brand-new, and he never got to use it. "I didn't mean to donate that." Spike removed it from the box as the worker took it. Spike threw the whoopee cushion into the bed of Gus's truck before getting in.

Gus drove to the other side of Bluesky and parked his truck in front of Warren Pritchard's house. In the back of the truck were sandpaper, two cans of brown paint, and two brushes. "Does Mr. Pritchard know we're coming?" Spike asked. "I don't want him calling the police again."

"That won't be a problem," Gus assured him. "Warren's happy that we're painting his woodwork. When I told him it was your idea, he called you a 'fine young man.'"

"Do you think the judge will count this as my community-service hours?"

"That's all taken care of." Gus smiled. "After we finish this job, your debt is paid."

Just as Spike and Gus were taking the materials out of the truck, Todd's Bronco pulled up behind them.

"I wonder what they're doing here," Spike said as Todd, Chase, and Andy got out of the Bronco.

"We're here to fix Mr. Pritchard's roof," Todd said. "I guess you kind of rubbed off on us with your Handy Helper gig."

Spike and Gus went to work, sanding the wooden window frames. Todd and his friends set up ladders and climbed up to the roof with tar and shingles. It was an especially hot day, and Spike could hear an occasional groan come from overhead. "Do you think they're okay up there?" Spike asked Gus.

"Sure, they're young guys. They'll be fine."

After a few hours, Warren came out on the front porch with some tall glasses of ice water. "Come on down, young fellas," he called from the bottom of the ladder. "You need a break. I've got some water here and some nice fresh peaches."

Chase and Andy were resting in the shade of one of the elm trees enjoying the cool refreshing water. Todd noticed Spike sitting on the porch steps munching on a peach. "I've been wanting to tell you something," Todd said, "something that's long overdue."

Spike looked up at Todd, unsure what to say.

"I'm sorry about giving you a hard time. At first, I was just joking around. Then I don't know what happened. Things got out of control. I've been a total jerk!"

"Yeah, I acted pretty stupid too."

"Maybe what we need is a do-over. What do you think?"

"That sounds fine with me. Hi, there. Name's Mike, but my friends call me Spike."

"Nice meeting you, Spike. I'm Todd."

Gus and Spike went back to work painting the window frames. They could hear Todd and his friends walking around on the roof. Once in a while, someone would let out a yell. "Probably hit his thumb again," Gus would say. "That smarts!"

At last, the workers stood in the street admiring their work. "Your house looks much better," Gus pointed out to Warren. "But you know what would help it even more?"

"What's that?" Warren asked.

"If you got rid of that No Trespassing sign!"

"That I can do!"

"I hope you don't mind if we make a stop on the way home," Gus said. "The Clawson sisters are having a little plumbing problem."

"The Clawson sisters?"

"Rose, Violet, and Daisy," Gus said with a grin. "Some people call them the Flower Girls."

"I can see why. Their parents must love flowers."

"Yes, they did. Rose was married, but her husband died several years ago. Now the three ladies live together. Violet and Daisy are what we used to call old maids."

Gus pulled up in front of a gray Victorian-style house with a peaked roof and gingerbread trim. It had a huge porch that went across the front of the house and wrapped around to the side. Rose bushes grew along the white picket fence and beds of daisies, bachelor buttons, and zinnias lined the walkway.

"Wow!" Spike exclaimed. "I guess they really do like flowers!"

Violet Clawson answered the door. She was wearing a bright fuchsia dress with a strand of pearls around her neck. The flower motif continued inside the house—pink mums on the wallpaper, vases full of flowers on every table, and even flowered floor coverings. Her sisters quickly joined her in the living room. "Good afternoon, ladies," Gus said. "This is my friend, Michael."

"Thank you so much for coming." Rose invited them in. "We are having a slight problem in the upstairs bathroom."

"Daisy dropped her teeth in the toilet," Violet whispered to Spike.

"I'll be right back," Gus said as Rose led him away up the stairs.

Spike stood near the door while Daisy fussed with the vase of flowers on the coffee table. She hadn't said a word since Gus and Spike arrived.

"She won't talk without her teeth," Violet said in Spike's ear. "She's so vain!"

"Michael!" Gus yelled from the top of the stairs. "Can you go get the wrench from my truck? They've got a little leak up here."

Spike was relieved to have an excuse to go outside. He climbed into the back of Gus's truck and took a wrench from the toolbox. In the bed of the truck, he saw the whoopee cushion he had thrown there that morning. Spike picked it up. It was almost too hot to handle after lying in the sun all day. Spike tucked it in his pocket and went back in the house with the wrench.

"I'll take it to him," Violet offered, taking the wrench from Spike's hand.

Spike sat carefully in one of the fancy high-backed chairs. When Gus came down the stairs with Rose and Violet, Spike stood up quickly, not noticing the whoopee cushion fall from his pocket.

"Okay, ladies," Gus said. "I think everything is fixed."

"Thank you so much," Rose walked with Gus and Spike toward the door.

"Oh, look!" Violet exclaimed. "Daisy, here's your hot water bottle. It's still nice and warm."

Before Spike could say anything, Daisy sat down on the chair he had just vacated. "Pfffbt" came from the whoopee cushion.

"Oh!" Daisy exclaimed. "Excuse me!" Daisy stood up and then sat down again. "Pfffbt" came from the whoopee cushion again.

Gus and Spike hurried out the door. "I guess I should have left the whoopee cushion in the donation box," Spike said as they got in Gus's truck.

"Why do you say that? Those ladies are gonna have fun with that whoopee cushion for days."

"It looks like you and Todd are getting along a little better," Gus commented as he drove Spike home.

"Yeah. He's not such a bad dude after all."

"So you think he's changed?" Gus asked.

"I don't know. Maybe I just had Todd figured out wrong."

The two rode along in silence for a while, and then Spike said, "You know something? It's really hard to hate somebody and pray for them at the same time."

"Is that so?"

"Ah, Gus. You knew that all the time!"

Everyone was excited about the tenth anniversary celebration of the swimming pool in Bluesky. But no one was as excited as Beth Anne. "We've been practicing so hard. I hope we win," she said to her teammates.

"But remember the Special Olympics oath," Willy said. "'Let me win, but if I cannot win, let me be brave in the attempt.'"

"Of course I remember it," Beth Anne said. "Sarah makes us say it at every practice."

The dedication ceremony was set to begin at two o'clock, followed immediately by the Special Olympics unified relay exhibition meet. In the meantime, the pool was open to the public with no admission charge. The pool was packed with kids splashing and diving and going down the slide. The lifeguards were all armed with monster soaker guns and were spraying any of the swimmers who asked for it. The other Handy Helpers were already in the pool when Chris came out of the men's shower room.

"Sorry, I'm late," he said. "I had to watch Tyler until Mom got back from shopping."

"What happened to your tattoo?" Melissa was the first to notice that the cobra was missing most of its head and all its tail.

"I guess it's wearing off." Chris looked at his shoulder. "I hadn't really noticed."

"Wearing off?" Logan asked, confused. "You mean it wasn't a real tattoo?"

"Naw, it was just a temporary one." Chris laughed. "You didn't think I would really get a tattoo, did you?"

"How about your grandma's tattoo?" Amber asked. "Was that a fake?"

"Yeah," Chris admitted. "Grandma just wanted to see what Grandpa would say if he thought she got a tattoo."

"He must have been shocked," Laura said.

"He's been married to Grandma Mo for forty years." Chris smiled. "And she still manages to surprise him."

"The mayor's looking good," Spike pointed out as Mayor Goodwin stepped onto the platform to begin the ceremonies.

"He should," Logan laughed. "He had four facials at the salon where my mom works."

"It took four facials to get the red dye off his face?" Chris asked.

"No, it only took two," Logan continued. "But it was such an improvement that he came in for two more."

"Citizens of Bluesky," the mayor said into the microphone, "it is my pleasure to unveil the new plaque that will hang on the front of this facility." With that, Troy Fillmore pulled away the sheet that had been covering the plaque. Everyone gasped as they viewed the large gold plaque with the words "Bluesky Aquatic Center. Dedicated by Mayor Marcus Goodwin."

Following the mayor's presentation, the swimmers on the Special Olympics unified teams were introduced. Beth Anne stood proudly next to her teammates. On the other side of the stage was the team from Marshallville. There were two girls and two boys dressed in matching swimsuits. "That's the team you could have been on," Melissa whispered to Beth Anne.

"I like our team. We're the best," Beth Anne said confidently.

The announcer led the swimmers in the Special Olympics oath and then asked them to take their positions. Brianna was the lead-off swimmer, followed by Willy and then Beth Anne. Melissa was last. The pressure would be on her to catch up if the team was behind.

As the whistle blew, Brianna dove into the water. Her stroke was smooth and quick. Melissa had given her some pointers that really paid off. As she reached out to tag Willy, she was still ahead of the swimmer from Marshallville. Willy was their weak link.

All they could hope was that he could finish his leg of the race. When he reached Beth Anne, the Bluesky team was far behind. Beth Anne used the breathing techniques she had learned and kept going as fast as she could. But it looked like there was no chance to win as she tagged Melissa.

"Go, Melissa!" the crowd was shouting as Melissa swam for all she was worth. The Marshallville team had also left their best swimmer for last. Melissa was able to make up some of the distance, but they were too far behind. The crowd let out a loud groan and then began to cheer for the Marshallville swimmer who grabbed the rope at the finish line.

"You did very well," Sarah told her team as they gathered outside the shower rooms. "You were up against a challenging team that has been practicing a lot longer. I'm very proud of all of you."

"I thought we'd win." Beth Anne groaned to Melissa and Brianna in the women's shower room.

"We finished the race," Brianna pointed out. "I think that's a lot considering a few weeks ago Willy couldn't even swim."

"We'll keep practicing," Melissa added. "We've come a long way, and we'll be ready in September."

Spike was taking the lawn mower out of the shed when he saw Todd come out the sliding door into the backyard. "What're you doing?" Todd asked.

"Mom wants me to mow the lawn." Spike moaned. "What does it look like I'm doing?"

"I thought you'd be getting ready to go fishing with your friends."

"Well, I can't. I have to mow the front and the back. With all this rain, the grass is really tall. It'll take me hours!"

"It just so happens that I have the day off, and I don't really have anything to do. There's nothing I like better than mowing lawns. Why don't you let me do it?"

"Are you kidding?"

"No, I mean it. Besides, it'll help me impress Jennifer, don't you think?"

Spike ran inside before Todd had a chance to change his mind. By the time Chris and Logan came riding up on their bikes, he was ready to go.

The boys chained their bikes to some trees and walked down the path to Fox Creek. As usual on a Saturday, lots of fishermen were seated on the banks. The boys looked past the boulders and scrub oak to the sandy beach farther down the creek. No one was in their favorite fishing spot.

Spike set his gear on a large rock and took something out of his bag. "Just what I need," he said, "peanut butter and jelly fish sandwiches."

"Are you eating lunch already?" Logan asked.

"You're going to eat jellyfish?" Chris questioned further.

"No, of course not." Spike chuckled. "I didn't say peanut butter and *jellyfish* sandwiches. I said peanut butter and jelly *fish* sandwiches. These are peanut butter and jelly sandwiches for the fish. It's my bait!"

OTHER BOOKS IN THE HANDY HELPERS SERIES

The Handy Helpers: A Rocky Start

Amber and her friends Laura and Melissa sign up to be junior volunteers at the senior center. But someone doesn't want them there and is sabotaging all their good work. Could it be the Three Handy Guys, three boys from their class who were already volunteering at the senior center? The girls fight back, and things get pretty messy until the seniors devise their own way to bring an end to the feud.

The Handy Helpers: Seven Is a Perfect Number

Melissa thinks that she is being pushed out by the new girl in town, Beth Anne. Even Melissa's best friends, Laura and Amber, seem to like Beth Anne better. When Beth Anne asks to become a member of the Handy Helpers, Melissa uses the fact that Beth Anne has Down syndrome as an excuse to keep her out. She says it will be hard for Beth Anne to do the Handy Helper jobs. When Beth Anne risks her life to rescue a dog left in the care of the Handy Helpers, Melissa begins to see things differently.

Coming Soon . . .

The Handy Helpers: Not a Happy Camper

The Handy Helpers are excited about going to summer camp—that is, everyone except Beth Anne. Her parents want her to go to a free camp for children with disabilities. Beth Anne begs them to let her go to camp with her friends. Finally, her parents admit they don't have enough money to pay the camp fees. When the Handy Helpers offer to help Beth Anne raise the money to go to camp, the problem seems solved. So why has Beth Anne suddenly changed her mind and wants to go to the special camp after all?

Edwards Brothers Malloy
Oxnard, CA USA
November 24, 2014